I0654029

# BETTER MANN

## TRACY GRAY

B. LOVE PUBLICATIONS

# Introduction

Dear Reader,

Once upon a time, I started a series called "Basketball Baes." At that time, in my indie author mind, I envisioned carrying that series out for as many books as I had storyline ideas. Then, there was a shift in the atmosphere, and I was invited to join a group of talented authors under an umbrella held steady and upright by B. Love herself. But what to do with these basketball stories that were left over from my time alone? Duh. Release them.

So, please enjoy the story of Omari Mann and Kitari Miller.

Kitari Miller is the older sister of Kirbie Miller. If you read my books, then you know that Kirbie is the main female character in *By Chance.* If you were wondering about Kirbie's family, and her relationship with said family... you're about to have all of your questions answered.

Thank you for choosing to purchase or download *Better Mann.* I really hope you enjoy it!

~ Tracy Gray

# PREFACE

From Tracy's Heart

*Better Mann* has a Tortured Soul/PTSD trope. That means that one of the characters has experienced trauma and now has a hard time trusting others.

Because of the trauma that Kitari experienced (off page, but described), this book is a slow burn with significantly fewer sex scenes than one would typically find in a Tracy Gray novel.

Violence perpetrated against women may be triggering for some readers. Please make sure to take the proper precautions to maintain your optimal mental health if you decide to proceed with reading this book.

# PROLOGUE

## KITARI

There was absolutely no worse kick in the ass than the kick in the ass that came when you agreed to something you didn't even want to do in the first place, and things went left.

That was one of over one million thoughts, running through my mind as I sat on the beach on the Caribbean Island of Iredia with a group of girls I barely knew... and definitely didn't consider friends.

They were the cast of *Grid-Iron Girlfriends*—a group of women who were either married to, divorced from, dating, smashing, or "co-parenting" with a professional football player. I wasn't a show cast member, even though my man played tight end for the Londynville Leopards. I was actually the "friend" of cast member Portia Johnson, who shared two children with running back Gavin Talbert.

At the moment, Portia was watching me with keen eyes, as the other cast members watched me with amusement, shock and/or disbelief. Hell, I was looking at the screen of Serita Underwood's big ass cell phone with disbelief, too. I could barely wrap my mind around what I saw on the screen, even though it was right there.

Right there on the "Celebrity Tea Time" blog were pictures from the wedding of Elijah Emerson and InstaChat model Mariah Freeman, which had taken place just a few hours earlier.

I stared wordlessly at wedding pictures of the man I lived with. The man I loved with. The man who had my heart. The man who was my future. Only now, he was clearly Mariah Freeman's future, because she was his wife. She carried his last name. All I carried was an incredible amount of pain, confusion, and disbelief.

"This motherfucker," Portia intoned between her clenched teeth.

"Why does he have to be a motherfucker, Portia?" Jennica Smith questioned.

She was my least favorite member of the cast, and there was absolutely no love lost between us. It was obvious by the way she always made it her business to make sure I understood she didn't respect or fuck with me on any level. She was always borderline rude and always, always had something smart to say out of her thin lips, anytime she deigned to speak to me.

Shrugging her shoulders, she added, "The heart wants what the heart wants... and obviously, it wants Mariah... today and forever."

Right then, I should've beat her ass, or at least punched her in her disrespectful mouth, but I couldn't. I was mesmerized. I couldn't pull my eyes away from the pictures of Elijah in his black tux and Jordans to even respond to Jennica's hating ass.

He looked so handsome, but even more than that, he looked happy. He stared into Mariah's face with unadulterated love and happiness. I literally felt the exact second my heart shattered. It wasn't slow or subtle. It was more like a rocket hitting a pane of glass. The shattering was complete. My heart was unsalvageable.

———

I wasn't sure how I got off the beach and away from the heifers that made up the cast. All I knew was that somehow, I managed to get back to the hotel room I was sharing with Portia and pack my belongings.

"We were able to get your ticket changed, Kitty," one of the producers of the show told me, calling me by my "stage" name. Clearly, Elijah had a type because I'd started my ascent into pseudo-celebrity as an *Only For Fans* model. When I first started my *account*, replete with photos of myself in lingerie, teensy bikinis, and booty shorts, I'd chosen to use an alias—Kitty Yum-Yum.

"I'm sending Alan with you." He wouldn't stop jabbering. "He'll be recording when you confront Elijah. We've got eyes on the ground, and we've been able to confirm that the couple will meet with their families for brunch mid-morning tomorrow at *Precise*, in Downtown Londynville, Kentucky. We'll have a car waiting to take you and Alan to the restaurant."

Nothing he said registered to me. I didn't care about the "blah blah blah" coming from his mouth. I just wanted to get back to civilization to see what I was able to recover of life as I knew it, before "*Celebrity Tea Time*" (literally) blew up my spot.

While I was hurriedly and haphazardly tossing pieces of clothing into my luggage, my cell phone rang. Hoping beyond hope that it was Elijah, with some explanation on his lips about the misunderstanding that had to have taken place, I answered breathlessly. "Hello?"

The voice on the other end of my phone wasn't Elijah's, but it was just as welcomed because it was coated in love and care.

"Niecy pooh, where are you, baby?" my aunt Ayana Truesdale asked.

And that question was what caused the levees to break and the tears to flow—the concern in my aunt's voice. I could barely respond to the question, as I choked on the gulps of air that my body was involuntarily taking.

"You're okay, sweetheart." She assured me softly. "Breathe. Breathe."

I focused on the calmness of her tone. "Eli... Elijah." I tried to say before I burst into another fit of sobs.

"I know what his pathetic ass did!" my aunt spat.

Ayana Truesdale was the owner and head queen in charge of *Engineered Excellence Sports Management Group*. It was her job to know what each and every professional athlete on the planet was doing at any given moment.

"All I want to know is where you are, honey. Where are you, and who is with you?"

After a few minutes, I was finally able to bring my emotions under control to the point that I could reply. "I'm in Iredia, in the Caribbean. I was with the cast of *Grid-Iron Girlfriends*, but I'm in my room packing right now."

"Who's in the room with you?"

I looked over to where the producer stood in the doorway of my room, clearly ear hustling. "One of the producers of the show."

"Tell his or her shifty, shady ass to get out of your room, right now. Then, I want you to make sure you're not mic'd, go into the bathroom, close the door, and turn on the water faucet full blast."

Once I was in the bathroom, with the door closed and the water running, I spoke. "I'm here."

"Why are you packing, Kitari Alise Miller? Where are you headed?"

"Home."

"To do what? Confront Elijah before he leaves on his honeymoon?"

"Yes," I admitted as tears began to flow again. "He owes me some answers, Auntie. Why would he do this to me? He's the one who encouraged me to come on this trip that I didn't want to come on. He's the one who..." I dissolved into hysterics as it dawned on me that he'd set me up. He'd purposely sent me out of the country so he could marry his bride in peace and not have to worry about me crashing his wedding.

My aunt True, as we called her, let me have my 'unhinged' moment. When she heard my sobs decrease to moans and whimpers, she spoke.

"Kit Kat, you're right," she told me. "That motherfucker definitely owes you some answers, but what I can promise you is that you aren't going to get them by popping up on him in front of his family and friends. His response to that would probably hurt and embarrass you worse than what he's already done. And what you surely won't do is agree to let some opportunistic producer record your humiliation for shock value and ratings. You are not that bastard's cash cow. You're not even a regular on that show. He doesn't get to make money off your pain. Let him know that you don't need his ticket. What you need is the love and concern that comes from family. I'm sending you a ticket to Chicago. Come home, baby. I'm getting my guest room ready for you. When you get here, I will love on you and help you figure out your new normal."

# ONE

KITARI

"Keetyn Alise Miller!" I called out. "You'd better be putting on those shoes, little girl. We're gonna be late for the birthday party."

My mini-me came walking into the living room, shoeless. "Mommy, it's not like Auntie Kirbie can fire you just because you're late. She'll be mad, but she'll still be your sister. Auntie Kinzie said that sisters are forever."

"Well, that's a nice sentiment, but I know Kirbie, and she would definitely fire me if we're late to Chayse's first birthday party. But we're not going to be late. We're not going to give her a reason to be mad or fire me as her sister. You're gonna run and put your shoes on before I give you the pow-pows." I demonstrated the swatting motion that was synonymous with her getting popped on the butt.

"Okay." She relented, making her way to the shoe rack that was by the front door of our tidy, but small condo.

The two-bedroom unit certainly wasn't the sprawling four-thousand-square-foot home I'd once shared with Elijah Emerson, but it was mine... and it was paid for. No one would ever have the opportunity to send the sheriffs to evict me from it, like Elijah did. As if the humiliation of him marrying old girl wasn't enough, he had me evicted from the home I'd lived in for over two years and got an order of protection *against me*... as if I was a threat to his well-being.

While my daughter put on her shoes, I picked up the present I'd selected for my niece. It hadn't been an easy task, as I had no idea what one got for the baby who had everything. Somehow, I'd managed to find something that I thought she would like.

―――――

My younger sister, Kirbie and her fiancé, NBA player Chance Parker, lived in a modest house by professional athlete standards, but the back-yard didn't owe anybody anything. Particularly because they had decked it out to look like a carnival on steroids.

My parents were under the tent where face-painting was happening.

"Hey," I said, going to my mom first, to give her a hug, while my father scooped up his granddaughter.

My father was the very definition of a *girl dad*. He had fathered three daughters, and those daughters, in turn, gave him two grand-daughters. He couldn't get a boy in his life for anything on earth.

He didn't seem to mind, though, as he traded kisses with my mini-me. When they finished sugaring each other up, I stole my father's attention from my daughter. "Hey, Daddy."

"Hey, Kit Kat." He pulled me into a side hug.

"Go put your present on the table, Kit Kat," my mother suggested. "Kirbie and Chayse are over by the girl who's blowing up balloons."

"Be right back," I assured them, while taking Key's hand and walking across the backyard, past the face painters, the girl making soft-serve ice cream cones, and the Disney Princess until we arrived at a booth where mylar balloons were being blown up.

"Hey, sis." I crooned in her ear from behind.

She turned around, giving me a bright smile.

Kirbie and I were often accused of wearing each other's faces. We both had our mother's deep hickory complexion as well as her striking hazel eyes and cavernous, attention-grabbing dimples. That was where the similarity ended, though. While Kirbie was tall—at least five feet nine or so—and thin like our dad, I was medium height—around five four—and curvy like our mom. She bent slightly to hug me, then handed me Chayse while she picked up Key's big self.

"Put her down," I chastised in between taking kisses from Chayse's sweet caramel-colored cheeks.

"Nope." Kirbie's shoulder-length tresses swayed back and forth with the movement of her head shaking in the negative. "No matter how big she gets, Key will always be my baby."

Key leaned over and blew a juicy raspberry on Kirbie's cheek. Her Aunt Kirbie laughed good-naturedly, while wiping the excess 'love' from her jaw.

Kirbie spotted the photographer they'd hired to get random shots. "Preston!" She waved him over to us, then moved her gaze to me. "Let's get a sister picture with the girls and get the girls together."

"No shots of Key, Kirbie," I reminded her for what had to have been the one millionth time.

In another life, when I was an *Only For Fans* Model, I lived to post pictures on social media. Once I had Key, I made it my business to withdraw from the internet. I didn't have any personal pages or accounts, and I did everything I could to keep my daughter's existence private. If you knew about her, you knew. If you didn't... you weren't supposed to know.

"Okay." She relented easily.

Kirbie knew that once I put my foot down, that was it. If I said I wasn't going... I wasn't going. And pictures of Key at the birthday party of NBA power-forward Chance Parker's daughter, was a total no-go. Those pictures would move through social media faster than the speed of light.

"Sister picture then?" she suggested.

I figured that it wouldn't hurt anything to post one with my little sister, on her daughter's big day. "Definitely." I agreed, moving closer to her.

Soon, we each had an arm wrapped around the other, and we were smiling with sisterly love.

"Perfect," Preston announced after getting a couple of shots of the two of us.

"Now mother and daughter." Kirbie gathered Chayse up and posed with her like she was Kim K., and Chayse was Chicago or North West or somebody.

"Say 'Kardashians'," I teased before Preston took the snap.

I would've loved to get a picture with my baby, looking as cute as she looked, but I just couldn't chance it. I kneeled so that Key and I were eye level, then I hugged her slim body to mine and kissed her peanut butter colored jaw. "I love you, Key," I whispered into her barrette and ribbon adorned hair. "I love you more than anything."

# Two

KITARI

The phone call came mere minutes after I'd dropped Key off at daycare. It was from an unsaved number that I didn't recognize, but from an area code that was all too familiar.

"Hello?" I asked, uncertainty in my tone.

"Did you honestly think that I wouldn't find out that you had my daughter? And now that I know, I won't allow you to keep me out of her life."

My heart started to pound overtime. "Who is this?" I asked, dumbly, because I knew exactly who it was. Four years had passed since the last time I'd heard it, but his voice was still familiar. It was his words that were throwing me off, though.

"You know who the fuck this is!" he spat.

"Yeah, I do," I admitted, equally as nastily. "What I don't know is what daughter you're talking about. I don't have any children that belong to you."

"Oh, here you go. Always with the bullshit, *Kitty.*" He spoke my alias with venom.

"Kitty is dead. She died four years ago. This is Kitari. Is there anything that *I* can help you with?"

"Bitch, I don't give a fuck—"

I hung up on him. If there was anything that Elijah should have remembered about me, he should have remembered that I didn't play the "bitch" game.

I didn't refer to myself as a bitch or allow anyone else to refer to me that way. Even "inner Kitari" knew not to refer to me as "bitch." She always addressed me as "boo." Even when she was cursing me out or telling me that I was fucking up, she addressed me as "boo." That was self-love. And I would be damned if I let somebody else talk to me in a way that I didn't talk to myself.

My phone rang again. This time, I was ready for him. "What the fuck do you want, number forty-five?" It wasn't lost on me that Elijah's jersey number was the same number as one of my least favorite former presidents.

"I want to see my daughter... tomorrow. You've kept her away from me for four long years. I want to meet her in person. After that, I want joint custody of my daughter... and if you try to fight me on it, I *will* sue for full custody."

"Sue for whatever you want to sue for," I said. "My daughter belongs to me. If you want children so badly, get your wife pregnant. It's been four years. What the hell are you waiting for? Your little peeny-weeny ain't got what it takes to fully shoot up the club?"

I chuckled because I knew for a fact that Elijah's equipment wasn't the largest. It got the job done, but it surely didn't leave any lasting... side effects and impressions. His little man definitely wasn't writing "Elijah was here" on no walls. It was barely touching them.

"Fuck you. When I get this DNA done, we're gonna see who's laughing."

"Eat a dick." I ended the call, making sure it had disconnected before I let the tears that were threatening to fall, breach my eyes and roll down my cheeks. "Fuck!"

Why couldn't Elijah just go along on his merry way and leave me and my daughter alone?

Four years earlier, he'd done everything in his power to rid himself of me. He'd sent me out of the country while he married another woman. Upon his return from his honeymoon, his first order of business was not spending time booed up with his new wife. No. It was to pull out all the stops on the "Kitty Yum-Yum Cancellation and Humiliation Tour."

He'd had me forcibly removed from the home I'd lived in for years. His family made sure I wasn't in any position to talk publicly about our relationship, our situation, or the details of his treatment of me. Meanwhile, he, his family, and his management team went on a media campaign that painted me as everything from a liar to a homewrecker, to mentally unstable, to a pariah, causing me to lose everything—most importantly, my livelihood.

He and his family had done everything in their power to ruin and break me. And they'd succeeded. They had made sure that my life was a blackhole. The only tiny bit of light that shined through during my lowest moments was the thought of my daughter. Now, he wanted her, too? Well, he wasn't getting her. There was no way in hell.

I hit Kirbie's name in my contacts.

"Good morning," she said pleasantly.

"I'mma need a lawyer," I replied. My voice was still quivering from the tears I'd shed.

"What kind, and how soon?" my sister probed.

The three daughters of Weston and Ramona Miller weren't as close as some sisters were. We tended to do our own things, have our own friends, and our own lanes, but you would be hard pressed to find three sisters who were more down for each other when crisis situations arrived.

"Elijah Emerson just called me."

"What the hell does he want?"

"My daughter."

"Well, too bad!" she spat. "He will never get his hands on my niece. I hope you told him that—"

I cut her off. "Of course, I did. I also told him that she's not his, so he has no claims to her."

"What did he say?"

"That he wants joint custody... and if I try to fight him on it, he'll go for full custody. I guess he thinks that I'll give him a DNA test."

"Right," she co-signed. "We'll get an injunction and keep his request tied up in court for years. By the time he gets through the red tape, Key will be old enough to say that she doesn't want or need him. And if he's so hot and bothered to claim her after all these years, why hasn't he been supporting her financially?"

I tried not to sigh. "I don't need him to support Key, Kirbie. She's not his."

No matter how many times I alluded to the fact that Key wasn't Elijah's daughter, my family always seemed to "poo-poo" me, like I was only saying that because I wished it weren't true.

"I know," she said quickly.

Too quickly.

So quickly that it let me know she was being agreeable to avoid my professing once more that Elijah Emerson was not the father of Key Miller.

"I'm saying hypothetically," she clarified. "If he thinks she's his daughter, why hasn't he come through with any bread?"

"I don't even know how he found out about her." I mumbled, but not quietly enough, because Kirbie heard me.

She sighed heavily before beginning with, "Don't get mad, Kit Kat."

"I'm already mad," I assured her, "because that's not how you start a conversation when you don't want somebody to get mad."

"I know. I know." She was repentant. "I was really hoping that nothing would come of it, but I saw some pictures floating around *InstaChat* and *FacePage* of Key and Chayse from the birthday party. Some of the guests—they took random pictures... like Chance's mother... and your mother."

Chance's mother, I could forgive. She didn't know me or my rules about never ever posting photographs of my daughter on the internet, but my own mother? She knew better.

"Your mother posted pictures of my daughter on *FacePage*?" I questioned.

"Oh, now she's *my* mother? When she's messing up, she's my mother. Any other time, I'm Daddy's girl, and you and Kinzie are

Momma's babies," she joked, although I wasn't in a joking mood... like... at all.

"You and Kinzie can have that lady if she's the reason that Elijah is calling my phone. I have one rule. *One rule*, Kirbie. Don't put pictures of my fucking child on social media. And she can't even respect that? She gotta be posting pictures of my child?"

Kirbie's voice was quiet and calm when she spoke. "In her defense, Kit Kat, and you know I don't defend Mom often, but in her defense, she only posted on her page, and you know I had Kinzie make it private for her. Mom is proud of her granddaughters. She thinks they're gorgeous, and worth bragging over. I'm sure he didn't see the pictures on mom's page. She would never do anything to invite Elijah back into your space. She knows how badly he hurt you by marrying old what's her face. Hell, she was the one who was willing to go to jail for the pleasure of killing him when he pulled that shit on you. It had to have been on Chance's mom's page."

"I'm too pissed to listen to reason, right now."

"Got it." She offered her assurance. "Are you headed into the office?"

Kirbie and I both worked at our aunt True's sports management company. Kirbie worked as a junior representative, which was basically a glorified assistant to a senior representative. She was currently earning her master's degree and creating connections and relationships. I had every confidence that my sister would one day be a senior representative herself.

I was a player liaison, which basically meant that when True's athletes signed to new teams in cities they were not familiar with, it was the liaison's job to connect them with their new communities.

If the client needed a place to live, I did the footwork. I met with the real estate agent and presented the client with a short list of options.

If they needed a new doctor, dentist, chiropractor, masseuse, trainer, physical therapist, I found a very short list of candidates for them to choose from.

If they needed a housekeeper, I had connections with all types of cleaning companies. Did you want one person to clean the spot? Two? Three? I could make that happen.

Need a daycare?

Babysitter?

Nanny situation?

Private elementary school?

Personal chef?

Kitari got you.

Aunt True had liaisons in almost every major city. I was one of three liaisons in the Midwest region.

"I have to meet up with Omari Mann." Omari Mann was an NBA player who had been traded to the Chicago Bison during the off-season.

Kirbie made some sounds that I couldn't quite decipher.

"What? What are those sounds about?"

"Nothing." She hedged before just admitting what she was thinking. "It's just that you and Omari Mann seem to spend a lot of time together. I'm saying, every time I turn around, you're off with him somewhere."

"Please, stop it." I rolled my eyes, even though she couldn't see me. "Tell it to Aunt True. She's the one who assigned me to him. It's not like we spend personal time together or even interesting time together. All we've done together so far is house hunt. And it's not my fault that he can't find a house, condo, or townhome he likes enough to pull the trigger on."

"Are you sure he's not procrastinating on finding a place to live so he can keep spending time with you? Maybe you're the *trigger* he's trying to pull."

I couldn't help laughing aloud at that.

"Omari Mann is gorgeous."

"Omari Mann is like... thirty-five years old," I reminded her.

"And you're twenty-eight. What's the big deal?"

"Would you date a thirty-five-year-old man, Kirbie?" I probed.

"It's not about whether I would date a thirty-five-year-old man, sis. It's about if I would date somebody seven years older than me, and the answer is yes. I mean, Chance was thirty when he got me pregnant with Chayse, and I was only twenty-four. So... yeah. I would. Besides, Mann wears his age well. He's definitely got that distinguished gentleman mood down. Close cut fade, super neat, and crisp mustache and goatee.

You know what I can't stand? When men have struggle beards that are all... I don't know... just not right. Mann's facial hair is... let's just say that thang is thangin."

"Uh, do I need to let Chance know that you're on my phone gushing about Omari Mann?"

"Why are you trying to choose violence this morning?"

We both chuckled.

"I'm just sayin', big sis."

"And I'm just sayin'—Omari and Kitari? Nah, I don't see it for him... especially with our names rhyming and stuff. That's like... the definition of doing too much."

"Or it could be the definition of kismet. Y'all's names rhyme, Kit Kat. That's cute."

"Quit trying to sell me a dream, Kirbie. Dating a professional athlete is something that I never plan to revisit. And I mean, *never*! Besides, I ain't got time to entertain no dudes. I'm too busy trying to raise Key. She needs all of my attention, and she's not used to sharing me... nor should she be. I'm all hers, and she's all mine."

# THREE

OMARI

Apart of me didn't know why the hell I kept making this girl go visit houses with me and the realtor. I wasn't even sure if I planned on buying a property in Chicago.

I was thirty-five years old, had a one-year contract with the Bison, and with my track record as an NBA journeyman, I felt pretty certain that it wasn't going to be renewed at the end of the season. Who wanted a thirty-six-year-old taking up space on their roster and in their salary cap, when they could have a young buck with young knees and young elbows?

I sure in the hell didn't want to settle down in Chicago if I wasn't going to be playing ball. Not that there was anything wrong with the city, per se. It had all the attractions, entertainment, crime, and drama that one would expect from a big city.

The weather was just too damn mercurial for my liking. It was a sweltering soup pot in the summer, and as cold as Antarctica in the winter. I was more of a Pacific Northwest person, when it came to weather. People complained about the rain in Seattle and Portland, but the temperatures were way more moderate... and consistent. It was sixty degrees in May, and sixty degrees in December. I liked that.

Anyway, there was another part of me that knew exactly why I kept making Kitari Miller visit houses with me and the realtor. She was just too fucking pretty, and I liked looking at her. I liked having her right next to me—going in and out of kitchens, offering opinions in that sweet, but sultry voice of hers. I liked walking behind her, watching her ass sway, smelling the alluring fragrance that always seemed to follow her. I liked her laugh. And the way she rolled her eyes when she saw an element in a property that she couldn't stand. I liked to see her hazel eyes light up when she saw something in a property that she adored. I liked the juxtaposition of those light brown eyes against that chocolate-coated skin.

Her light tap against the window of my truck brought me out of categorizing everything that I liked about Miss Kitari Miller. I looked over at her and couldn't help the smile that bloomed on my face. I rolled down the window.

"Good morning, Kitari Miller."

"Good morning, Mr. Mann. You ready to see this place?"

"Yeah." I agreed, then turned off the ignition and popped the locks. I slid my left leg out to the sidewalk, then unfolded myself from the truck, taking a moment to discreetly adjust my clothes and my dick.

"It's pretty, and you can't beat this location," she commented, looking up at the brick edifice that was fashioned in a way that reminded me of the New York City brownstones on the Upper East Side.

It was new construction, on a very discreet block just steps from Lake Michigan.

"From the pictures, it seems like the primary bedroom looks out on the water."

She had a dreamy expression on her face.

"So, water views are your thing?" I probed, standing over her.

At six feet eight, I was used to being much taller than people, particularly women. I liked that Kitari almost always wore heels; they gave her some height and made her legs seem to go on for miles. I took in the little dress and high heels she was wearing.

"Yes," she confessed, before giving me the eye. "But we're here to see if water views are *your* thing."

"Lead the way." I stuck out my arm so that she would walk in front of me.

She started to sashay, then turned and faced me. "Don't think I don't know that you just wanna watch my ass."

"Nah, little mama." I shook my head in disagreement. "It's not your ass, it's the sway of your hips that causes my imagination to run wild. I mean, you got a nice ass... and I do like watching it. But having a fat ass gives me very little information. That sway, though... it lets me know exactly what type of time you're on."

"What type of time am I on, Mr. Mann?"

I raked my eyes over Kitari's full frame. It was obvious to me she was double-minded about me—all men, probably. I could tell she'd been through something, even at her young age. The fact that she'd been broken by some careless motherfucker and put back together by her own hands and design basically radiated from her. Still, I knew there was a part of her that was digging me. She didn't think I noticed, but I saw how frequently she eye-fucked me.

Kitari wasn't a carefree, bubbly twenty-something that had nothing but time and opportunity to trick off with. She didn't spend her evenings or weekends having "girls' nights" or even dates with dudes she met on dating sites. She wasn't on her *City Girl* shit.

Kitari spent her free time with her daughter. She was a dedicated mother. I knew, because when she was first assigned to me, I would reach out to her to run around, seeing places with me on the weekends. She let me get away with it a few times before she laid down the law. Told me that her weekends were for her baby, and no client, not one, would be given the opportunity to pull her away from what was most important to her... her daughter. I respected that. I respected her.

Kitari was professional. She didn't try to be cute in my face or bend over in front of me, giving ass shots or cleavage shots. She always dressed in a way that covered her assets but caused my imagination to wander. She kept it light and friendly but rarely gave me the opportunity to cross the line into sexual innuendo.

Still, she was all woman, and I was definitely all man, which meant that there were times when our oppositeness—her feminine to my masculine—became apparent and unavoidable, like now. Plus, there was the fact that I wanted her... spread wide and butt-ass naked in the middle of my bed.

"I'm not fucking wit' you right now, Miss Miller."

She chuckled.

We walked up the stairs together, and I rang the doorbell. A few moments later, my realtor, Dominique Atkins, swung open the door.

Dominique was everything that Kitari was not. She liked to flirt... rubbing up against me, putting her titties in my face.

Dominique's aggressiveness was probably another reason I always brought Kitari with me. I needed her there to act as a buffer.

Dominique was true to form—she ignored Kitari while giving me the brightest of Colgate smiles. "Hey, Omari," she drawled.

"What's up, Dominique?"

She grabbed me by the hand, still refusing to acknowledge Kitari's presence, and pulled me into the home's foyer.

"You're gonna love this one, Omari." She gushed. "You felt like the last couple of places we've seen were too big for a single guy, such as yourself." She bumped her shoulder against my bicep playfully, before she continued. "This one is only thirty-two hundred square feet, spread out on three floors."

When she used the term "spread out," my mind and eyes couldn't help but go to Kitari and how badly I wanted *her* spread out. I quickly wiped the smirk that was threatening to overtake my features away, but not so quickly that Dominique didn't catch it, along with my glance at Kitari. Kitari, on the other hand, was oblivious.

Dominique's pretty features morphed into an unpleasant frown. She rolled her dark brown eyes. "Yeah, so uh, this one has thirty-two hundred square feet, three bedrooms—"

I cut her off. "Let us look around. If I like it, you can give me all of the details."

"I'll give you anything you want, Omari." She flirted. "All you have to do is ask."

The sigh that escaped my lips was heavy. "Listen, I'm not exactly sure what I've done to make you feel like this is a situation for you to shoot your shot. I'm honestly looking for a crib, not for... anything beyond that. I'mma need you to let me rock on all this flirty shit." I paused briefly, while making direct eye contact with her. "Can you do that?"

Kitari spoke for the first time since we'd come into the house. "Because if you can't, Ms. Atkins, there are plenty of realtors in the Chicagoland area who would jump at the opportunity to work with Mr. Mann. And who would be a bit more professional than flirting with and rubbing up against him at every given opportunity."

It was written all over Dominique's face that she wanted to clap back at Kitari. As I stood there and waited to see what the play was, I decided if she even so much as responded to Kitari, her ass was fired.

"I'll let you two look around. I'll wait here in the foyer for you." She spat through clenched teeth.

"Let's go see if the views from the primary bedroom live up to the pictures." Kitari grinned at me.

And just like that, looking into those deep-set, piercing hazel eyes of hers, Dominique Atkins was forgotten.

Because the property was a brownstone, the stairs were right off the foyer. I followed Kitari up two flights of stairs, mesmerized by the way her ass and hips moved the entire way up.

"Oh my gosh, Mr. Mann," she said once we'd reached the top floor. "Stop watching my butt." She rubbed both hands over her ass, and I couldn't help laughing.

"This girl." I shook my head back and forth while she treated me to a dimpled smile.

"I'm just kidding. Needed to break that tension from... downstairs." She motioned down with her head. "I'm glad you finally called Miss Dominique on her unprofessionalism. It's like with each place we see, she gets more and more bold. At this rate, she's just gonna pull out your junk at the next showing."

"My junk?" I parroted back to her.

She had the nerve to blush and look away from me. "You know what I mean."

"I do." I agreed. "And on that note, let's check out this view."

"Are you gonna seriously consider this one, Mr. Mann?" she asked me as the two of us traipsed across the carpeted floor of the landing and made our way into the primary bedroom. The bedroom, the adjoining bathroom, and the walk-in closet were the only rooms on the floor.

I gave her a noncommittal shrug of my shoulders, glad that she didn't push. Instead, she walked right over to the French doors that let in an insane amount of natural light and led to a balcony that overlooked a nice-sized sliver of Lake Michigan. It certainly wasn't a full-on view of the lake, but it was enough to know that you were looking at it. And with the way the property was situated, the balcony was semi-private. It was only large enough for two or three chairs, a table, and very minimal decor, but it was a nice retreat.

Kitari leaned on the railing, closed her eyes, and held her face up toward the sun. I watched her silently. She was prettier than a motherfucker, but she was unavailable. She made that obvious. She gave off hella *unavailable* energy.

"Do you even realize how gorgeous you are?" I asked, softly.

Her hair was in a ponytail, and as the breeze kissed her, it made the strands that had worked themselves loose of the ponytail holder blow easily.

"And this is the most relaxed I think I've ever seen you." I continued.

"It's the water. I'm a total water baby, and a sunflower, too. Two of my most favorite things in life are the sun and water."

"What are some others?"

"My daughter, my family... shopping." She laughed and opened her eyes.

I smiled at her, then walked back into the bedroom.

After Kitari and I had checked out the house, we found Dominique in the foyer, right where she said she'd be.

"What'd you think? I mean, what did *you all* think?" She stressed the words, "you all."

"Yo... it's... cool," I stated, after hesitating.

Kitari shook her head. "This was a really good find, Dominique. I really like the property, and truth be told, I think Mr. Mann liked it as well."

"Well, the builders are only doing seven units... and in this location, you can imagine that they're hot properties. If you really are interested, I wouldn't procrastinate too long, Omari. Three of the units have already sold. Also, keep in mind that only two units have this layout. If you like this floorplan, you should definitely move faster, rather than slower. Not to rush you or put any pressure on you," she added.

"Nah, I get it. That's information that I need if I'm really interested. Thanks."

"You're welcome."

"We'll be in touch," Kitari assured her.

The two of us left the property and headed to our respective vehicles. Kitari glanced down at her watch.

"Hey, Mr. Mann," she began.

I cut her off. "What I'd tell you about that Mr. Mann shit when it's just the two of us?" I questioned.

"You know I'm trying to keep things professional, Mr. Mann."

"Things are professional, Kitari," I assured her. "We spend too much time together to be so formal. Besides, I call your sister by her first name. Yo, I call your aunt by her first name, and she owns the whole shit."

"Okay." She finally relented. "What I was saying before you so rudely interrupted... Omari, was that I have a few hours before I have to pick Key up from daycare. Do you wanna grab something to eat and talk about the place we just saw?"

I didn't necessarily want to talk about the place, but I was open to spending more time looking into her pretty face. "Yeah, let's do that."

———

Kitari and I rode in my truck to a little Mexican restaurant that she recommended, not too far from where the property was located. We were seated quickly and handed menus.

"What do you recommend?" I asked her before I even cracked the menu.

"I always get the fish tacos, because I love fish tacos, and because they make them with Alaskan salmon." She rolled her eyes toward the back of her head, in an imitation of sexual pleasure.

I froze momentarily. "Ay, don't ever do that again. Unless..."

She giggled, and I decided right away that I liked the sound. "Sorry. It's just that Alaskan salmon is everything. Their chicken tacos are really good, too. The steak ones, too. Shoot, everything here is really good. Both the homemade salsa and guac will make you want to slap your abuela."

We both chuckled.

"Do you drink?" I asked her. "Are the drinks any good?"

"Uhm, I don't really drink. I'm saying, I'm a single parent, and I need to be cognizant and aware at all times when it's just me and my baby. So, I've never had their drinks, but whenever I come with my sister and her guy, he gets the beer."

I nodded, then opened the menu and perused.

Once the waitress had taken our orders and collected the menus, we sat there in a comfortable silence for a little bit.

Finally, I glanced over at my companion. She met my gaze with curiosity blazing in the hazel eyes that intrigued me so much.

"What's the deal with you, Omari?"

There was no preface to the question.

"I get the distinct impression that you aren't really interested in purchasing a property." She continued. "What I can't figure out is, why you're wasting Dominique's time like this."

I took a sip of the beer I'd ordered.

"I'm not trying to waste her time."

"Well, I'm glad you spoke up today. No shade. But I was starting to think that the reason you kept seeing properties, when you know you aren't interested in purchasing, was to get close to Dominique. I kept wondering, A, why am I here, and B, why doesn't he just man up and ask the broad out? So, what's up? You a commitment phobe?"

"How long have you been working for True?" I asked, curving her questions for the time being.

"Uhm, about two and a half years." She took a ladylike sip of her water.

"You know much about sports?"

"I know some," she admitted. "Enough to have a real conversation... and real opinions."

"You know what a journeyman is? An NBA journeyman?"

"I do." She nodded. "And I know you've played for nine teams in your fourteen-year career."

We fell into silence again, as I debated with myself whether or not to open up to her. After a few moments, I filled the empty space with my words.

"I've packed up my life and my belongings eight different times since I was drafted and moved to whatever market was willing to play me and pay me. I've sold five properties. Sometimes, it's just easier to pack up your shit without all of the fanfare of having to stage and sell a house, or a condo or a townhome. Sometimes, apartment life is just easier." I sighed. "Besides that, I'm at the point where I might be ready to hang up my Nikes. I'll be thirty-six next year. I'm not too enthused by the thought of dragging my almost forty-year-old body up and down the court for an eighty-two-game season."

The waitress returned with our food and placed the dishes on the table, warning us to be careful because both the plates and the food were hot.

Once the waitress was out of earshot, Kitari decorated a taco with the salsa and guacamole she'd bragged on, then took a healthy bite.

"Stop feeling sorry for yourself, Omari," she chastised once she'd finished chewing. "Dikembe Mutombo played until he was forty-two years old. And we won't even talk about Vince Carter." She paused. "Oh yeah, we will talk about him. He played until he was forty-three. Forty-three years old, Omari. And here's you... whining when you're only thirty-five."

"Okay." I acquiesced since she'd called me on my shit. "Let's keep it a buck. I don't know if I feel up to packing up my life and moving it across the country twenty-five more times at the age of thirty-five." I bit into one of my carne asada tacos and tried not to flip the table over, because the taste was out of this world. "We're gonna have to start a dinner club or something." I looked at her over the top of my taco. "Because you're good at picking out restaurants."

"Thank you." She returned to the topic at hand. "I get it. It can't be easy having to learn new cities, make new connections, assimilate into a new community, only to have to pick up and do it again at the end of each season. That has to make a person feel very... transient. I get that it must be hard to put down roots when you feel like every move could be or will be temporary." She polished off another taco. "But Chicago's a cool city. It might be worth having a place here."

"Chicago's weather is trash," I said matter-of-factly. "This place is too hot in the summer and too cold in the winter. It ain't for me. I grew up like this, and I promised myself that once I got out, I would never come back." I shook my head empathetically. "I'm not here for the Midwest... like, at all. This is my least favorite part of the country, like my literal least favorite region." I braced myself because one thing I knew was that it was never cool to shit on someone's hometown. That was particularly true for Chicagoans who tended to love their city with a rabid fierceness.

"Where'd you grow up?" she asked.

"Beloit, Wisconsin."

She giggled, and I really liked the sound. "Yeah, that's like Chicago adjacent."

"Don't flip the table for what I'm about to say," I cautioned because I felt like it was necessary. "Beloit is not Chicago adjacent, baby." I looked around the restaurant, then lowered my voice. "Fuck the Bears. Green Bay Packers for life."

Her pretty face fell, and for a millisecond, I wished that I'd kept my mouth shut. "You root for the Green Bay Wackers?" she clarified.

I didn't respond, but apparently, I didn't need to, because she'd heard enough.

"I don't believe this." She mumbled, shoving the last of her taco into her mouth before collecting her purse. She scooted to the edge of the booth we were sitting in. "I've spent weeks... months running around town, being seen with a cheesehead? I can't believe this."

I watched in silence as she stood up from the table. "Ay, Kitari..."

"What? What, cheesehead?" She snapped.

"Wow," I stated. "Let me just pay, and we can get out of here. I'll..."

She started to laugh as she fell back into the booth. Her hand was over her mouth, and her shoulders shook with amusement.

"That shit wasn't right," I told her once I realized that she'd been playing with me.

"It wasn't, but that's how Chicagoans act, isn't it?"

"Are you setting yourself apart from other Chicagoans?" I questioned.

"Not at all. I bleed blue and orange for the Monsters of the Midway. I still revere Michael Jordan, and I think the Cubs finally winning the World Series was one of the best things to ever happen. I'm all about the Sears Tower and the Mag Mile and the South Side. I love pizza—could eat it every day. I'm Chicago, baby. But," she shrugged her shoulders with practiced nonchalance, "if you wanna root for that buster ass team, who am I to judge you?"

"Buster ass team?" I repeated. "Newsflash, your Bears can't seem to ever beat my buster ass team. When's the last time the Bears won a game against the Packers?"

"Who cares?" She waved me off with a delicate hand. "I'm not about to argue over what I know is a fact. What's understood doesn't need to be explained. The Bears are a better team. Always have been. Always will be. They belong to the better city."

"Whatever." It was my turn to wave her off.

"Tell me what you thought of the place we just saw, Omari. It was really nice. If I could afford it, I would buy it right out from under you."

"Word?" I recoiled, my hand on my chest in fake incredulity. "That's what we're doing? We're just saying whatever?"

"You're the indecisive one." She batted long, curly eyelashes at me. "I'm very decisive."

"Oh yeah?" I eyed her.

She met my gaze. I liked how she did that occasionally, even though she was closed off. She still gave me that feminine energy that I liked, even though both of us knew she wouldn't act on it. "Very," she reiterated.

"I didn't like the carpet," I confessed.

She nodded encouragingly. "What else didn't you like?"

"Counter heights and showerhead are too short, but ain't much you can do about that."

"Maybe—" she began.

I cut her off with a shake of my head in the negative. "Nah. I customized a house for my height once. I loved living in the house. It was the most comfortable house I'd ever lived in. Everything fit me. But that house was a nightmare to sell. What person of typical height wants seven- and eight-foot shit? Nobody. That's who. When I decide where I want to retire and settle down, I'll customize that property. But I'm not customizing a temporary space."

"Cut to the chase, Omari. Are you going to consider the property? Are you going to consider making an offer?"

I eyed her suspiciously. "If you were me, would you make an offer?"

"If I was me... with money, I would make an offer, Omari. I mean, it's way more space than Key and I could ever need, but still. It's a beautiful place."

"Is Key your daughter?" I probed.

She nodded.

"Is Key her real name or her nickname?"

"It's her nickname. She's Keetyn Alise Miller. I wanted to name her after me... without naming her after me, if that makes sense. We call her Key."

"Is it spelled K-E-Y?"

She nodded again.

I studied her. "There's a story behind that name, huh? When I think of a key, I think of something that unlocks something. Did your pregnancy unlock something in you?"

"My pregnancy was very... difficult." She rolled her eyes and stuck her tongue out at what I assumed was the memory. "But when Key came, she was the key to my heart and the key to the city of Kitari. When I first considered the name, I couldn't stop thinking about the Stevie Wonder album that my parents used to play all the time, *Songs in the Key of Life*. When she was born, there was no other name that would've fit everything she brought into my life and my situation. She turned some very dark days bright, just with her presence. She's the key of life."

"Yo, God was a beast for sending her to you then."

"He was." She whispered her agreement with a head nod. Her eyes were bright with what looked like tears.

"Do you get weepy just from talking about her?" I asked with a genuine smile, because that had my heart thumping.

"I get weepy just thinking about everything she means to me." She dabbed at her eyes with a napkin from the table. "Sorry. One day, maybe I'll tell you my story."

"Cap," I stated simply. I didn't believe that she would let me get that close to her. Kitari was a walking '*closed for business*' sign.

"Can't keep it bottled up forever. Gotta tell somebody eventually."

"Okay." I acceded with a nod before changing the subject. "There is nothing like a mother's love, especially when your mother is a single mother. I'm saying, if she's your only parent... then her love is your existence. Your daughter is lucky to have you."

"Were you raised by a single mom?"

"I was. And they say a woman can't raise a man, but my mom damn sure did. The love she poured into me meant everything. Honestly, I think it was her love and her faith in me that propelled me to success. She buoyed me and wouldn't let me fail, no matter how hopeless things seemed. No matter how fucked up things were, she was right there, cheering me on... believing in me." I paused. "Maybe one day, I'll tell you *my* story."

"I know the house is pricey, but I think you should make an offer." She held up her hand when I started to respond. "Even if you don't stay with the Bison or stay in Chicago, think of it as an investment. You might not enjoy Chicago. You might think the teams are trash and the weather's trash, but a home with a view of Lake Michigan, in that neighborhood in Chicago... that's always gonna be a good investment. You're always gonna make a return on your money."

# FOUR

## KITARI

I hadn't seen Omari Mann in a little over a week, and when I was honest with myself, I could admit that I missed him. I figured he'd decided to put an offer on the brownstone, because I was certain that he would've summoned me to visit more places with him by now if he hadn't.

I missed his energy.

And the way he looked at me.

And the way he made me very aware of my own femininity and its effect on the opposite sex.

"Dammit, Kirbie." I mumbled, remembering how she talked about Omari and me being kismet because our names rhymed. I stomped into my closet to pick out something to wear to Aunt True's annual birthday barbecue—something that I wanted Omari to both notice and like, without looking like I was trying to dress for him.

I wished that Kirbie had never put him on my mind like that. Now that she had, all I could think about was how fine he was; how he actually did have the look of a distinguished gentleman... who would flip me over and fuck me inside out; how his perfectly groomed mustache and goatee would look so good buried between my thighs. "Shit." I fanned myself with my hand, which did nothing to cool me off.

I grabbed my phone and quickly pressed the contact for Kirbie.

"Hey, sissy." She crooned into the phone.

"What are you wearing to Aunt True's thingy?" I asked with no preamble.

"Uhm, high-waisted denim shorts and some type of off-the-shoulder, cropped, short-sleeved sweater from Celine or Cerene or somebody. You know I hired a stylist, right? Chance likes to make public appearances, and I'm hard to fit. I got tired of being dragged on the internet and accused of having no style, so I hired Hadley Johns." She paused. "Uhm, you're asking me for fashion advice on what to wear to Aunt True's *annual* party? The same party you've been to for the last two years? Does this have something to do with Omari Mann?"

I completely deflected. "How do you think Mom and Dad are gonna handle having both Key and Chayse overnight?"

She let me make it and didn't call me out on changing the subject. "Yeah." She chuckled. "I don't know. I guess the same way they handled having you, me, and Kinzie. You know they're professionals at handling that little girl energy. Plus, they probably have some over-the-top grandparents-only crap planned."

"You're right, because whenever Key comes back from spending the night with them, I have to deprogram her. Those grandparents let her do anything she wants." I took a beat. "How are you feeling about letting them keep Chayse? Letting Mom keep Chayse?"

Growing up, Kirbie and our mom weren't what one would consider... close. Our mom kind of shunned her and acted like she couldn't relate to or understand Kirbie.

My sister was a bit of a tomboy who found more pleasure in working in the garage with our dad than she did in shopping at the mall with our mom, like Kinzie and I did.

Even when Kirbie finally confessed her pregnancy with Chayse, our mom had given her more grief than acceptance. Because of that dynamic, Kirbie leaned more on Chance's mom for that mother-daughter bond than she did with our mom.

Chance's mom loved Kirbie almost as much as she loved Chance.

She'd relocated from her home in Nashville to Chicago to be a live-in caregiver for Chayse. There was never a need for our parents to keep Chayse. She had her Nana Jackie. So, this was our parents first time having the opportunity to get Chayse overnight.

"I'm good with it. Mom seems to love and enjoy Chayse... It's me she can't connect with."

"Kirbie—"

"Don't start, Kit Kat. It's taken a year of therapy for me to face some ugly truths. Mom and I don't mesh well. Daddy is my guy—my rock, my source of parental love and acceptance. That's why children need two parents." She sucked in a deep breath. "I didn't mean that, Kit Kat. Children need love. It doesn't matter if they have two parents or one parent. They need love."

"No worries," I said dismissively. "I didn't take it personally, because I know exactly what you meant. You did need Daddy in your life. I mean, we all did, but like you said, he's your main source of parental love and acceptance. I'm glad he was there to give you what you needed, little sis."

"Me, too. But you changed the subject ten minutes ago. Is this desire to dress a certain way for Aunt True's thing about Omari Mann? Say yes, Kit Kat. I really want it to be. I love the thought of y'all together."

"You love the thought of us together?" I repeated. "Why?"

She sighed heavily. "I see something there. I have a gift, you know? I can always see couples before they happen. I saw Gensie and Cross getting together the first time I saw them interact. The chemistry was... palpable. She didn't see it, though. Told me that I didn't know what I was talking about. Now look at them... all married, with those twins, and another baby on the way. I also should've told her that the boy was gonna keep her pregnant. I swear Cross is trying to lock her down for the next two lifetimes." Chuckling, she continued. "Anyway, you and Omari make something inside me tingle, and that's my sign. He's your future, big sis."

"I really wish you would stop saying stuff like that, Kirbs. You've got me thinking about him in a whole other way, now. He's a client; I need to be on my professionalism when it comes to him. I can't go out like some groupie chick."

"Cross was Gensie's client. All that alone time together on their *professionalism* is probably what led to him busting it wide open."

We both chuckled.

"Besides, you won't have to go out like a groupie. I can assure you that Omari will be very amenable to taking things from business to pleasure," she told me.

"Whatever, ma'am. What should I wear to Aunt True's thing? Help me! Sundress? Ass-hugging jeans? Ass-hugging jean shorts? Capris? A ball gown? What?"

"Let me get Hadley on the line. I'm gonna pay for this consultation, but you owe me."

———

Hadley Johns didn't play any games. A few hours after speaking with her and showing her the contents of my closet, via a video call, a delivery arrived at my condo. I ripped open the packaging and rifled through the selections right there at my front door.

Initially, I was torn between two options. The first was a casual Nike swoosh T-shirt dress that I knew I could make look super chic and edgy with the right accessories and my Nike Dunks gym shoes. The second was a tiered, short, white number by *& Other Stories* that was fresh, feminine, and completely flirty. In the end, I settled on a printed mini dress that featured puff sleeves, a tie at the waist, and a hem that barely tickled my mid-thigh. It was the perfect collab between feminine, flirty, stylish, and effortless chic that I was hoping for.

"Look at you, being all gorgeous and putting every other woman here to shame," was how my sister greeted me when I joined her and Chance on the spacious stone patio of my aunt's lakefront mansion.

Aunt True owned several homes, but the lake house was the one she used to host her annual birthday party.

She was cute, calling it *her* birthday party. She was never the guest of honor. Everybody who'd ever attended knew that True used the gathering as an opportunity to celebrate her clientele—to shower them with accolades, recognition, and appreciation.

"Not every woman," Chance Parker said, intimately nuzzling Kirbie's jawline, like we weren't in the middle of a crowded patio.

"Chance." My sister giggled, swatting playfully at her fiancé.

"What?" He mumbled, his face still buried in hers. "You're fine as fuck, and you're mine."

Kirbie giggled again, sinking into him.

I watched them.

*I want that*, I thought to myself. I wanted somebody to love me publicly and claim me out loud.

I tore my gaze away from them because it was too painful to watch, knowing that I probably wouldn't get that. It was hard enough finding a dude that would love me and treat *me* right. Now, I had Key to consider. He would have to accept and love Key. But even more than that, he couldn't be no nasty motherfucker that was only trying to get close to me, to get *close* to my daughter—one of those sick mother-fuckers who touched little girls... and did more than just touch them.

I sighed. *I'm gonna be single until Key goes to college*, I told myself.

"Was this the only thing you decided to keep from the selection Hadley sent you?" Kirbie asked, bringing me out of my own head and back to the present.

Chance had walked away to join some of his teammates.

"It's so cute, and this... what is this, pink? This pink is everything against your skin, Kit Kat. Trust you to elevate it even more with the straw hat and straw bag." She tapped the brim of my hat. "And a bucket hat, no less. You're too damn chic for me, big sis."

I pretended to model for her. "Yes." I hit a pose. "Yes." I hit a different one. "Yes." One last pose.

"Come through, Kit Kat." She hyped me up, until she was distracted by her phone. She looked down and quickly read the text. "That's Gensie. She and Cross just arrived."

"Well, since Mom and Daddy have Key, I think I'll find a cocktail to sip on," I told her. I knew Kirbie would never try to exclude me just because her friend showed up, but I also knew that she and Genesis were a "twosome" not a threesome.

"You don't want to hang out with me and Gensie?"

"Nah. You know I love Gensie, but she's your friend."

Once upon a time, I had a friend circle of my own. Somewhere between taking up with Elijah and having things end with Elijah, their priority in my life slipped and kept slipping. Now, my only friend was Key. But I believed what the professionals and the books said—you really shouldn't try to be friends with your child. So, I guessed that meant that I didn't have any friends.

"See you later." I leaned in and gave her a strong hug, before walking away.

Once I was at the bar, I requested a margarita. While I waited for the mixologist to make my drink, I shot a text to Omari Mann.

**Me:** Hey, are you at this party?

A few seconds later, his response came through.

**Mr. Mann:** Yep. I'm over here in the cut, watching the most gorgeous woman I know prove that there is no competition.

**Me:** Is Dominique Atkins at this party?

**Mr. Mann:** Get the fuck outta here, Ms. Miller. You know I'm talking about your pretty ass.

I chuckled lightly at his flattery.

**Me:** This dress must really be flattering. You're the second person to refer to me as gorgeous since I arrived.

**Mr. Mann:** Trust. It has nothing to do with the dress.

**Me:** If I'm so gorgeous, don't make me do this party by myself, come find me. Keep me company.

**Mr. Mann:** I ain't gotta find you. I told you, I'm looking at you.

"Your margarita," the bartender said to me.

I reached over to take it from him, with a pleasant, "thank you."

"You child free tonight?" Omari asked, sliding easily to my side.

His cologne wafted down to my nose, encouraging me to look up at him. Omari Mann was a beautiful person. Physically, he put me in the mind of Method Man—just caramel colored, sexy, and attractive for no reason.

His voice, though. That was DMX, all throaty, raspy, rough, and aggressive.

*Uhm, wonder if he barks before he slides inside the pu...*

"I see you sippin'." He continued, bringing my thoughts away from wondering about his sexual proclivities.

"I am." I took a quick sip of the drink, to cover my amusement, then hummed my appreciation for the cocktail. "I'mma need more than one of these, so it's a good thing that my parents have my baby."

"You out here looking to get completely drunk or what?" he teased with a sexy grin.

"I'm just looking to get nice." I took another sip. "So, what'd you decide about that last property we saw together, the one with the lake view? I'm assuming you put in an offer, since my presence hasn't been requested at any more showings."

He nodded his head. "Yeah, I put in an offer. You were a better salesperson than Ms. Atkins. You might want to consider going into real estate."

"Seems boring," I admitted. "I like what I do. It's so varied. One day, I'm helping you find a house, the next I'm helping another athlete find a physical therapist. On another day, I might help somebody find a doctor. I like helping people find things that make their transition to a new team and a new community go a little bit more smoothly."

"I can tell that you dig your job." He took a beat, before adding, "Plus, you're good at it. I mean, like I said, you were a better salesperson than the salesperson."

I chuckled.

"I was gonna call you this week because I wanna take one more look at the place. You down to do that with me next week?"

"Yeah, I'm down to do that." I agreed. "As much as I hate to admit it, I've missed hanging out with you, Omari."

He pulled me into a hug that I could only describe as... platonic. "Let me find out that you're feeling ya boy."

*Definitely feelin' you,* I thought to myself as I tried not to audibly sniff up his fragrance, like I was doing a line of coke or something. "Well, hanging with you does get me out of the office."

"So, you're using me?" He squeezed me more tightly, but no less friend zone-esque. But when he leaned closer to me and whispered in my ear, "That's cool; you can use me up," the hairs on my arm stood at attention, and a tingle tap-danced down my spine. Things were certainly no longer friendly.

When he released me, I kept my drink in one hand and took his with the other. "Let me show you something."

We made our way through the throngs of people until we came to the perimeter of the backyard. At the security fence, I entered the security code and pushed it open.

"Oh shit, secret passageways. Now you've got me curious as to where you're taking me. You're trying to get me alone."

I laughed out loud at his teasing while making sure to close the gate behind us. "You're crazy."

The expanse of Aunt True's private beach lay before us.

"Nah, you're crazy if you think you're about to get me into Lake Michigan. I don't mess with water."

"Nobody's getting in the water, scaredy cat," I joked. "We're just gonna chill on the dock. Come on."

His hand still inside mine, the two of us walked over to the covered, wood plank dock. I released his hand, only to swipe the Wet Wipes from my bag that I brought with me everywhere since I'd given birth to Key. We wiped down the two Adirondack chairs, before sitting.

Lake Michigan was calm, just sending ripples of water toward the shore. It was peaceful, and the weather was perfect.

"Okkaaaaayyy." He dragged out the word. "You got me out here doing romantic shit with you, baby girl."

He was right. Sitting on the dock, watching the water in matching Adirondack chairs with him was romantic.

"But it's obvious that you aren't open to nothing romantic, so... mixed signals much?" He called me out.

I choked on a sip of my liquor. "Well, damn, Omari. Is that what we're doing? Just saying that type of stuff with no precursor? No warning?"

"I'll never apologize for keeping it a buck with you. What's the play, Kitari? Are we cool business associates, friends... more?" He looked out at the horizon, quiet for a few beats. "We got a comfortable vibe. You occasionally do your little flirty-girl shit. I match your energy... within reason, never taking it further than you seem willing to take it. I do my thing—tell you that you're gorgeous, compliment the frame you're carrying... and you let me. You ain't reported me for sexual harassment or nothing to Kirbie or her boss... or True. What's the play, Kitari? More of the same, or is this... different?"

First, I set my empty cocktail glass on the dock beside my right foot, then I dropped my head into both of my hands.

"You're dramatic," he commented with a chuckle.

"My life is dramatic."

"Whose isn't?" he deadpanned.

"If you knew my story, Omari, you would understand my reaction better." I took a deep breath and focused my attention on the beauty of the lake in front of me. "I have literally been through the wringer."

"Yo, we have that in common," he mumbled. "More of the same, then. 'Cause you ain't ready for how I give it up, and I ain't ready for another woman who ain't ready."

———

I could not get that phrase out of my mind: *You ain't ready for how I give it up, and I ain't ready for another woman who ain't ready.*

"What do you think he meant by that?" I questioned Kirbie, who was on the other end of my phone while I scrounged around on the floor of my closet, looking for the mate to the shoe I wanted to wear.

"What do *you* think he meant?" She gave the question right back to me.

When I didn't respond, she filled in the silence.

"I think he meant that you aren't ready for him, and he's not trying to waste his time," she said.

"I like him, though." I mumbled before loudly saying, "Yes!" As I finally found the mate to the white, raffia high heel that was the perfect dupe for a Bottega Veneta sandal that I loved but could not afford.

"Unfortunately for you, *you've* always been the coy, sexy, mysterious sister, and *I've* always been the straight shooter. I've always just said whatever and let the chips fall. So, my advice would probably be trash. Maybe you should call or text Kinzie... or Mom."

I couldn't stop the scoff as it flew from between my lips. "Mom? Take advice from a woman who's been married to and carrying a compulsive gambler for the last twenty plus years? I don't think so." I stood from my closet floor, smoothed down my dress, and slid my feet into the shoes. I took a few quick snaps of myself and quickly texted them to Kirbie.

"You're so pretty, Kit Kat," she said after viewing the photos. "Regardless of Omari saying that he's not ready for another woman who's not sure of herself, he won't be able to resist you."

"The same way that mean-ass Chance Parker wasn't able to resist you, since we look just alike?"

"Exactly." She giggled. "You talked that man into buying a whole house. He bought a piece of property on the strength of your recommendation. Go 'head and woo dude."

"I haven't wooed a dude since... " my mind went back to a time long ago, "before I had Key, and I don't like thinking about or remembering that time in my life."

I had never told Kirbie... or really anybody about my time with Elijah... and particularly *after* Elijah. And I wasn't about to start. All my family knew was that whatever had happened to me after Elijah married Mariah Freeman wasn't good. They knew that it had changed me... and that I never talked about it. They also knew I came home from my stint in Londynville, Kentucky, with a brand-new baby, but not much else. They didn't push, but it wouldn't have mattered if they did. I couldn't see a time in life where I would be willing to give voice to things I'd experienced.

She agreed quickly because my family took their cue from me. "Right. Just be Kitari, and you'll have him eating out of the palm of your hand."

I sighed softly. "We'll see, Kirbs. Let me finish getting ready so I can pick up Key from school and meet Omari at the property."

"I can't believe you're letting him meet Key."

"You act like Omari and I are dating, and I'm finally introducing Key to him." Chuckling lightly, I continued. "It's not like that. Today was the only day that I could do this visit to the property with him, and this is the only time he could do it. So, little Miss Key will be in attendance."

"Well, have fun, and kiss the key to my heart for me. And tell her that Chayse and I are expecting a sleepover at our house soon."

"Maybe when Chance has his first away-game of the season, we can have a sister/cousin sleepover," I suggested. "We can even invite Kinzie."

"That sounds good, Kit Kat, but that's at least two months out. I mean, training camp doesn't even start until next month. I need my Key-time now." She pouted.

"Okay. Okay. Let's plan it for the weekend after next." I locked the door to my condo and started down the stairs of my three-story walk-up building. "I'm heading to the car. We'll talk later."

———

*This man is so damn fine, I don't know whether to be mad about it or happy about it*, I thought to myself.

I was mad about it because he wasn't mine. And I knew that eventually, there would come a time where all that masculine beauty would belong to some other chick. I was happy about it because it gave me something so freaking nice to look at every time I was with him.

"Mommy." Key wrenched me brutally from my thoughts with her sweet, innocent voice. "Is that man waiting for us?"

She gestured toward Omari, who stood in front of a luxury brownstone. He was wearing slightly oversized shorts that hung easily off of his waist (and showed off bowed legs), a mocha-colored T-shirt that matched his skin with the word KASI on it, low-cut white socks, low-cut white and mocha J's, and a backpack. He looked good enough to put on a spoon.

"He is," I told her as we came to a stop right in front of him. "Key, this is Mr. Mann. He's one of my clients at work. I've been helping him find a house, and I think he's gonna choose this one. Omari, this is my daughter, Key."

Omari graced us with a smile bright enough to light up a nighttime sky, and I tried not to swoon in front of my child.

"First of all, hello, Ms. Miller. Thanks for coming." He gave me a very quick hug, which mainly consisted of him leaning toward me, without actually touching our bodies together, and giving me a few pats on the upper shoulder region. "Second, it's nice to meet you, Key." He engulfed my baby's small hand in his own and shook it gently.

"You're just as pretty as your mom," he told her. "Are you smart like her, too?"

Key nodded, her eyes wide with wonder.

I wasn't sure if her wonder was about Omari's considerable height or his considerable fine-ness.

"Are you taller than a dinosaur?"

Omari laughed aloud at that, and even I couldn't help chuckling. Kids really did say the craziest things.

"Nah, I'm not that tall." He shook his head in the negative. "I am pretty tall, though, huh?"

Key nodded, her eyes never losing the wonder. "Yes, Mr. Mann. You're the tallest man I've ever seen. My granddaddy used to be the tallest... and Uncle Chance. But now you're the tallest." She paused, taking a beat before asking, "Would you pick me up so I can see how it feels to be that tall?"

Now it was my eyes that were wide with wonder. Key wasn't big on men. The only men she'd ever taken to had been my dad and, to a lesser extent, Chance Parker. Other men, even when we were out in public, she kind of shied away from. I wasn't sure if it was a read or vibe she picked up from me, based on my wariness and weariness concerning men, or if she had her own thoughts and ideas running around in her little mind. But her inviting Omari into her space two seconds after meeting him was... odd.

Omari was looking down at me, his sable-brown orbs questioning if I was cool with him picking up my daughter. I nodded slightly, and he turned his attention back to Key.

"Come on, little mama." He scooped her up into his arms.

Key reached her little hands toward the sky, giggling the whole while about how she could almost touch the sun. "I'm so close, Mommy. I can almost touch it. Lift me up more, Mr. Mann. Put me on your shoulders, like my granddaddy does."

"Key..." I began, but it was useless, because Omari was already doing her bidding. Before I could get any more words out, she'd been hoisted onto his shoulders.

I looked up at her, at least two feet away from me, and at least seven feet off the ground. I began to get dizzy. Not Key, though. She was having the time of her life, while I prayed that Omari Mann didn't drop my daughter to her death.

"I got her," he assured me, but his words did little to alleviate the nausea I'd started to feel.

"Omari," I began, and again, he was moving before I could get the rest of my words out.

"Elevator down, little mama." He brought her from his neck back around to the front of his body. "Your mother isn't comfortable seeing you up that high, that far off the ground, or that far away from her protection."

Key reached out her little arms to me, and I took her from Omari, holding her close, and dropping kisses on her sweet face.

Taking my face in her hands, she stared into my eyes. "I'm sorry for making you scared, Mommy. But you can be scared and still be brave, just like Thomas the Engine says."

I kissed her on her button nose. "I love you so much."

"I love you, too." She returned the kiss.

I looked up at Omari and found him watching us, his eyes soft.

"You ready?" I asked him, placing Key's heavy butt down on the ground.

"Let's do it."

Key held up her arms to Omari. "Pick me up, Mr. Mann... Just don't put me on your shoulders anymore because that scares Mommy."

He picked her up, then turned from me and jogged up the stairs. I followed, decidedly slower. After entering the lockbox code that I was sure Dominique had shared with him, he gained access to the house.

We walked into the foyer, and I looked around. "This is not the same unit that we looked at initially, right?" I probed.

"It's not," he admitted. He started up the stairs, Key still in his strong arms and me following hot on his heels. "If you remember that one, the top floor with the bedroom was carpeted."

I looked around at the white oak, hardwood flooring. "This is nice," I shared with a head nod. "Really nice."

"But this, in here," he stood in front of what I assumed was the primary bedroom, "is really why I chose this unit."

He disappeared inside the room, and I brought up the rear. The

primary bedroom in this particular unit was orientated a little differently than the unit we'd originally visited. From where I stood, just
inside the room, I could see the balcony, and not only that, but an
almost full-on view of Lake Michigan, in all her late summer glory. And
in the words of my youngest sister, Kinzie, "that thang, was thanging."

"Oh my goodness!" I exclaimed, not running but walking fast as hell
past Omari and Key, making my way over to the balcony door.

I could hear Omari's chuckles as I pulled open the French doors and
stepped outside. I was so mesmerized by the view of the water that I
didn't notice the table and chairs on the balcony that had been set for a
meal until moments later.

"Omari..." I began.

He stood there with a shy grin and my daughter in his arms. My
heart began to flutter and thump. My breath caught in my lungs, and a
shiver ran through my body.

He was holding my daughter in his arms, like she was his. And my
daughter was resting there, against Omari's—what I knew had to be—
strong chest, like he was hers and she belonged there.

The level of fear that seeing the two of them like that induced, was
only rivaled by the precious sentiment that seeing the two of them like
that induced. Still, I wanted to get the hell out of there. I wanted to grab
my daughter and get the hell away from Omari Mann and any other
man on earth that made me feel things... because feeling things was how
I'd gotten my heart shattered. Feeling things was what led to the myriad
of bad decisions I'd made. It was how I'd ended up as a single mother.
Feeling things was for suckers.

But before I could act on the fight or flight response that was
echoing inside my mind, Key's words came back to me. *You can be
scared and still be brave.*

Could I really be brave? Could I really push past the intensity of the
fear I was feeling and not run out on this man? I wasn't sure, but I
decided to give it a try.

"What is all this?" I asked, my voice as shaky as my smile.

"Afterschool snack." He shrugged his broad shoulders. "Once you
told me that you were meeting me right after you picked up little mama
from school, I figured she would be hungry."

All he did was bring food. *How can you be scared to eat with this man? You've eaten with him before. Once he puts Key down, it will be just like it was when y'all ate tacos together,* I coached myself. *Please stop being ridiculous.*

"I'm starving," Key announced, bucking in his arms until he took the hint and placed her down on the floor. "What are we having, Mr. Mann? I like peanut butter and jelly best."

"Word?" he questioned, looking into her hazel eyes. "Because I heard that you like seafood salad best. Especially seafood salad made by... I think she called herself your Tee-Tee Gensie."

"Auntie Gensie's seafood salad!" My daughter celebrated by doing some hip hop moves, with her arms held high in the air, then she broke that down into Crip Walking. And that was when Omari lost it, laughing until tears breached his eyes.

"Keetyn Alise, no, thank you! You have no business Crip Walking!" I scolded.

She looked stunned that I'd interrupted her celebration and stopped her mid-Crip Walk. "My Auntie Kinzie taught me that dance."

*I'm whupping Kinzie's ass,* I thought to myself.

Aloud, I said, "I'm going to talk to your auntie about that, but in the meantime, no Crip Walking... please."

She looked so deflated that I almost felt bad, but then I remembered that, as her mom, it was my job to set the standard. And I didn't think it was appropriate for my four-year-old to be doing a dance associated with gang members. Besides, there were any number of dances that she was allowed to perform.

Omari caught her eye. "You wanna help me put the food out on the table?" he offered.

Her spirit immediately reinflated. "Yes!" She danced around some more, but this time, she kept it cute.

"Come here and let me clean your hands with a Wet Wipe." I grabbed the pack of wipes from my purse, taking out one for Key, one for Omari, and one for myself.

When their hands had been wiped, and I'd given them each a squirt of hand sanitizer, I let them head to the balcony to set up the food.

While they were doing that, I texted Kinzie in the group chat that I had with her and Kirbie.

It was then that I let her know that I was beating her ass if she ever taught my daughter anything as inappropriate as Crip Walking again in life. Silently though, I had to admit that focusing on Key's dance moves distracted me and kept me from freaking out at the thoughts that Omari's mere presence had me entertaining.

**Kinzie:** Ugh, get the stick out ya ass, Kit Kat. I've been having Chayse C-Walking since she was fresh out the womb, and you don't see Kirbie tripping.

**Kirbie:** Right?!?! My baby be getting it. She be hitting isolations and spelling out her name and everything.

**Me:** Your baby just learned how to walk yesterday. Quit playing with me. I'm being serious.

**Kinzie:** I repeat...Ugh!

**Kirbie:** Anyway, aren't you supposed to be occupied eating seafood salad and whatnot?

**Me:** Why do you know about that?

**Kirbie:** Duh! Gensie's my best friend. When she gets a request about Key's favorite foods, you think she doesn't call me?

**Kinzie:** Wait, I was distracted. Who is she having lunch with? And who is she introducing to my niecy-pooh?

**Me:** The same Niecy-Pooh that you're trying to recruit into a set at 4 years old?

**Kirbie:** Clearly you're hangry.

**Kinzie:** Right!?!?!

**Kirbie:** Go eat some seafood salad, enjoy Omari's company, and let's talk tomorrow.

**Kinzie:** Who is Omari?????

**Me:** Bye, young heifers.

**Kinzie:** Bye, old hoochie

**Kirbie:** Bye sisters.

I slid my phone into my purse and met Omari and Key out on the balcony.

# FIVE

I couldn't decide if I was surprised or not when Kitari invited me to an event. The day we saw the property together with her daughter, I felt a small shift in the atmosphere. Where Kitari was once a walking '*closed for business*' sign, she seemed to now be sparingly offering a few hours of operation. She was still closed as hell... mostly, but there was a sliver of interest on her part now. I wasn't sure what brought about the change, but I was rolling with it.

She'd invited me to the closing banquet of a summer sports camp. A family friend, Maddox Mayhew, was a professional football player who held a camp in his hometown every summer for boys between the ages of ten and fourteen. When the program was over, Maddox apparently held an over-the-top banquet for them, complete with the mood of the ESPYs. According to Kitari, it was a formal, black-tie event, featuring golden trophies, acceptance speeches, delicious food, professional athletes, and fanfare.

I dressed the part, wearing a beige Tom Ford suit. When I arrived at the door of her condo, she didn't disappoint. She looked radiant in a navy, off-one shoulder number that was flowy and loose-fitting, yet still managed to accentuate every curve she was holding.

"Hey," she said softly and shyly. I wasn't even sure if she realized that she was batting her eyes or not. Kitari just had a way about her that was ultra-feminine. It wasn't anything she did purposely or even knowingly. Her way of being simple caused my way of being to react to her.

"Hey, beautiful." I took her in slowly but fully. "You look gorgeous."

"Is that him, Kit Kat?" a second feminine voice asked before the door swung open further, revealing a mocha brown young lady, wearing a ponytail and braces. She favored Kitari but wasn't her spitting image, not like Kirbie was. She did share Kitari's hazel eyes, though.

Before Kitari could respond, the young lady had moved past her and joined me in the hallway. "Hey. I'm Kinzie, Kit Kat's younger sister." She introduced herself.

"Ohhhhh," I nodded slowly, "the dance teacher."

She looked confused, so I gave her a few steps of the C-Walk.

Her face bloomed with a huge smile, showing that she also shared Kitari's deep dimples. "Your tall ass can dance." She looked me over appreciatively. "What's your name, Zaddy?"

"Take your hot behind in the house and watch my daughter, Kinzie." As an afterthought, she added, "and don't teach her anything. Just watch her."

Kinzie rolled her hazel eyes. "Introduce me to your date before you go, Kit Kat."

When Kitari didn't make any moves to introduce me to her sister, I did the honors myself. "What's good, Kinzie? I'm Omari Mann, a friend of your sister's."

"Watch my daughter, Kinzie," Kitari repeated again, which caused me to wonder if Kitari even needed to leave little mama with Kinzie if she had to be repeatedly reminded to watch the little girl.

"Stop acting like I don't know how to babysit," she huffed out. "Have fun. It was nice meeting you, Omari Mann."

"You, too," I said right before Kinzie pranced back into the unit, slamming the door behind her.

"Stop slamming my damn door!" Kitari fussed to the closed door.

"You cool?"

She turned her gaze on me, took a deep breath, and threw back her shoulders. "It's been a long day. I love my little sister, but she's young, and she has young-girl ways. Let's just say she plays too much and leave it at that. You ready?"

"Let's go."

————

Kitari had not lied when she said that Maddox Mayhew pulled out all the stops for his camp's end of the summer banquet. I was impressed with the entire setup. The red carpet, the production, and the celebrities —both local and national—who were in attendance. Maddox Mayhew really poured into the young guns in his camp. The entire thing was impactful. So impactful that it had me thinking about doing something like that for the kids in my own hometown, which if I stayed in Chicago would be even easier to pull off, since Beloit was only a two-hour drive away.

Maddox had extended an invitation for a late private dinner to Kitari and me. She'd declined, citing the fact that she needed to get home to relieve her babysitter. I would've enjoyed getting a chance to speak to dude about what it took, both financially and timewise, to pull together a summer clinic for kids, but I was just as cool leaving with Kitari.

"Thanks for the invite," I told her, once the two of us had settled into my Range Rover. "That was nicer than some team banquets I've been to."

"I know, right? It seems like every year, he improves it. It's getting more and more elaborate."

"Do you come every year?"

"I've been coming for the last three years or so. I'm not sure how long he's been putting it on, but I love it. I love seeing the kids all swagged out, being celebrated in all of their black-boy joy and stuff." She giggled.

"Word." I agreed, distractedly, because my mind was working. "Does Mayhew have a foundation, somewhere I can donate?"

I could feel her eyes boring into the side of my face. I glanced over at her before I pulled away from the valet stand.

"What?" I questioned, easing my way into traffic.

"Nothing, I guess. I just think it's... cool that you want to donate."

"Yeah. Kids need to be celebrated. They need to feel *seen*. Especially kids who look like us. And it can't be cheap to put on a production of that magnitude."

"I'll ask True to reach out to Maddox," she assured me.

A companionable silence fell over us that I filled with the sounds of the truck's stereo. "All I Need" by Method Man, featuring Mary J. Blige, came through the speakers. Even with the volume of the music, I still heard the light giggle come from Kitari.

With a tap of the controls on my steering wheel, I lowered the volume. "Why are you giggling?"

"I don't know. It's just a coincidence that I always think to myself that you remind me of Method Man, now I get in your truck and you're playing Method Man."

"I remind you of Method Man?" I repeated, mentally conjuring an image of the legendary rapper in my mind. I could give her that we shared the same medium brown complexion, the same mustache and goatee/beard setup, but otherwise, I didn't see it. "Whatchu know about Method Man?"

Shrugging her shoulders, she replied, "I don't know. My mother is this... humongous Wu-Tang Clan fan. I grew up with The Wu. I think Ghostface Killah is her favorite, but I've always been partial to Method Man."

"Method Man," I mused, then asked jokingly, "What is it that you think we have in common? You think we both have big dick energy?"

"Maybe," she teased back with another giggle.

There she went, doing that thing that I liked again, being all feminine and flirty.

———

The more time I spent with Kitari, the more time I wanted to spend with Kitari. And since I'd made the offer on the property and was just waiting for my closing date, I couldn't use house hunting as an excuse to see or spend time with her anymore. That meant that I had to boss up and ask her to hang out with me. That was what I was thinking as I busted out my last set of leg presses.

"Ah, I like the way you're following through with the whole range of motion, O. What're you doing? Did you come to Chicago to play some basketball or something? Did you come to be a problem for all of these young motherfuckers that think niggas your age can't hang? What're you coming to do, O?" My teammate and workout partner, Gideon Show, taunted me as he mimicked my motions with leg presses of his own.

"Fuck some shit up." I pushed the words out as I finished the set. I moved over to the barbells and prepared for the next exercise.

"Ay, who was that fine ass chick I saw you plastered all over *InstaChat* with?"

Since I hadn't been photographed with any woman except Kitari, I knew that was who he was talking about. Photographs we'd taken at Maddox Mayhew's banquet had hit the internet.

Who was Kitari to me? She was definitely a woman I was interested in seeing more frequently. She was a friend... kind of.

"She's a friend." I lifted the weight. Positioning my feet hip-width apart, I took a second to make sure my weight was properly balanced.

"What kind of friend? 'Cause lil yeah is bad as hell. I might have to come through and upgrade her, show her the difference between a young vet and an... old ass vet." He walked over and joined me at the other set of barbells that had been laid out by the gym's employee.

I generally liked Gideon. Not that I knew him all that well. I was new to the team; he was a vet, and we'd been paired together to meet up for a few off-season workout sessions. He was cool. He was arrogant and self-centered as hell, but cool, nonetheless... until he started his shit talking.

I didn't bite, though. I was well aware of the type of time Kitari was on, and it wasn't looking for a loud-mouth, narcissistic ass dude. Some dumb motherfucker had already taken her through the wringer and left her alone to raise their daughter. She didn't need a dude that was looking to trophy her until he got tired of playing. She needed somebody who would provide a sense of stability. She needed somebody who would come alongside her and help her with her shorty.

A teammate.

A protector.

A gentleman.

"Fuck around and pull a muscle thinking about old girl," he joked. "You need to focus on these deadlifts, my nigga. Later for reminiscing about ass."

He was right. As much as I enjoyed thinking about Kitari, I couldn't let her become a distraction, particularly not while I was working out. It was tough enough being the oldest dude on the team. The last thing I needed was to be the oldest dude on the team and the injured motherfucker. But I did decide that if I couldn't stop thinking about her, I needed to make my move sooner rather than later.

————

A few days later, Kitari sat next to me while I signed the closing documents for the house with the lake view. I'd asked her to have lunch with me after the closing, since it was her cajoling that convinced me to even buy the place. She offered to attend the closing with me.

When I'd shown up with Kitari, I could tell that Dominique almost swallowed her tongue. She probably would've put it on her momma that Kitari and I were fucking, but, of course, she would've been wrong. Not that I would've minded fucking Kitari, but for the time being, I just liked her energy. It was bright as hell, and I wanted it around me as frequently as possible.

Like for instance, when Dominique placed the keys to the spot in my palm, Kitari squealed happily, clapping her hands, and then throwing her arms around me for a hug. Her excitement was contagious, because I found myself chuckling and grinning my ass off, when closing on homes was some shit that was old as hell to me.

"Congratulations!" Kitari told me with a bright smile.

I watched Dominique watching her, before I responded with a smile of my own. "Thanks, pretty lady."

Kitari's phone rang, and she stepped away to answer it, while I gathered up all my paperwork from the table.

"So, are y'all a couple?" Dominique questioned softly. "Was that *professional relationship* thing y'all were pushing while we were house hunting just for the optics or what?"

I let my eyes meet hers. "Fall back, shorty. You just made a very nice commission off the fact that the woman you keep mean-mugging convinced me to buy this spot. That's really all that should concern you. You did your job. Have a nice life."

I stood then walked over to Kitari, who had just finished up her phone call. "Where should we eat?" I questioned.

"Let's go see the house first," she suggested, the bright smile giving me a front row seat to the dimples that lived on each side of her face.

"We've seen the house a hundred times, ma." Reminding her of that fact did not deter Kitari.

"I wanna see it one hundred and one times." She took a deep breath. "Clearly, you don't realize how much of a love affair I'm having with your new home."

I cocked my head to the side. "How do you do that?"

"Do what?" She was wide eyed, and her deep hazel orbs seemed to shine.

"Get me to do whatever you suggest?"

Her expression turned devious. "I really don't know why you've given me that power over you, Mr. Mann. But I promise you that I'mma use it to my advantage every time."


Two hours later, Kitari sat on my balcony, finishing her last California Roll. She adjusted her sunglasses, the drenching of her hickory-colored skin by the sun making it gleam.

"I used to date a girl with the most beautiful deep brown skin," I said into the breeze. "She hated the sun. Was always... running from it... trying to avoid it. She was always making some off-handed remark about how she didn't need to get any darker." I looked over at Kitari, taking her in with appreciation. "I love how you embrace it. You seem to bask in it."

"I understand her thought process," she admitted, "especially if she spent her life being teased, bullied, or ridiculed for having dark skin. I probably used to be the same way, once upon a time, like when I was still coming to terms with the fact that this is the skin I was given. I decided that I needed to figure out a way to love it... and myself. But now, I do love to luxuriate in the sun's rays... in moderation, and with sunscreen... with a high SPF. What feels better than the warmth of the sun kissing your skin?"

I looked at her over the top of my own designer shades. "You really want me to answer that question?"

Her burst of laughter was light.

"Damn." I shook my head back and forth a few times. "I really love the sound of your laughter."

It was her turn to look at me over the top of her sunglasses. "You'd better watch it, Mr. Mann. That's the second thing that you've told me you *love* about me in just a few minutes. You're blowing up my self-esteem a little too much."

"No such thing."

"Uhm, okay. Don't mess around and find yourself with a stalker," she joked.

"You? Stalk me? Shit, don't threaten me with a good time, mamas. But since telling you things that I like about you puts you in a good space, let me give you one last tidbit. I really love your energy, Kitari. It's light, and... easy. It's peaceful."

"You think so?" She looked away from me, and when she faced me again, she did so with a shake of her head. "Wow. Just wow. I never would've thought that about myself." She took a few beats. "I spent a period of my life in a very deep pit... a black hole. I didn't think I would ever be able to climb out of it. So, thank you for that, Omari."

If I wasn't mistaken, tears began to form in her eyes.

"Thank you for saying that. It's confirmation that I'm finding my way back to... Kitari, the Kitari I was before all of the bullshit tried to take me out."

"You're welcome, beautiful. Not only is it the truth, but I'm glad to give you the perspective of somebody on the outside looking in at you. I mean, that's not to say that you aren't closed off in some areas, or that there's not pain in your energy as well. I recognize that, and I don't want to downplay it. I just want you to know that what you give me... what I get from you when we're together... it's all good."

"Well, if we're being honest, that's because you make it so easy, Omari. Being with you is... breezy. You just give off this vibe that I can be myself around you, and you'll accept that. As somebody who was made to feel like they were never enough... I need that."

"Whoever made you feel that way is a dumb motherfucker, Kitari. And that's real." We sat there in companionable silence. She sipped her bottled water while I polished off the last of my salmon nigiri. Although I couldn't see her eyes, she seemed a million miles away. "You wanna talk about it?" I offered.

After pushing out a large sigh, she spoke. "You probably already know about it. You probably saw the whole thing play out on the internet... along with the rest of the world."

"Wait. The demise of your last relationship played out in public?"

"Yeah." She didn't remove her shades, but she was staring so intently at me that I could still feel the heat from her gaze. "Me. Elijah Emerson. Kitty Yum-Yum. *Grid-Iron Girlfriends.*"

I shrugged my shoulders because I had no idea what she was talking about. I mean, I knew that Elijah Emerson was a professional football player, and I knew that there was a reality show called *Grid-Iron Girl-friends,* but I had no idea where she fit into the equation.

"You don't remember me being dragged all over and through Beyoncé's internet?"

I shook my head. "When was this?"

"Four years ago," she confessed softly.

My eyes went wide in realization. "Wow. It seems like we were going through our shit at the same time. Four years ago, I was enduring my own much-documented dragging on *Beyoncé's* internet." I tried making light of the situation, although it was anything but light. "I went through a very public, very hostile, very ugly divorce. I was trying to keep my head above water, so I missed you almost drowning in your own drama."

"Wow," she repeated for the umpteenth time. "That's wild. We were getting dragged at the same exact time." She chuckled lightly but with little humor. "We have a lot in common, Mr. Mann."

"Oh yeah?" I questioned. "Tell me about it."

"First of all, our names."

"Our names?"

"Uh, they kinda rhyme. Omari? Kitari?"

I chuckled. "Well, there is that."

"We could never get married with our names rhyming like that. Can you imagine the hell we would catch? Or the invitations? *Your presence is requested as Omari and Kitari join their lives together*," she mocked.

"You think about marrying me, Kitari?"

The gasp stole her breath for a moment.

"You can tell the truth, mamas," I teased, bringing a bit of levity to the situation. "It's obvious that you want the kid."

"You're crazy." She snickered, shaking her head at me. "Actually, I don't think about marrying anybody, especially not while Key is little. I'm not one of those mothers who values men over the safety of her child. It would take a special man to get me to trust him around my daughter. Having said that," she lifted her shades and eye-fucked me a little bit, "you do... make me wonder, Mr. Mann."

"Wonder what?" I looked out at the lake, waiting to see if she would keep it one hundred with me, or if she was gonna feed me a half-truth, or even straight-up bullshit.

"I don't know." She hedged.

"Yeah, you do." I took a sip from my own bottle of water.

"Okay." She huffed. "I wonder what it might be like to date you, to get close to you. I mean, you're really easy to be around, Omari. You never... do too much. I appreciate how you don't act thirsty for the coochie. I'm in a space where I'm trying to get back to me. I'm relearning myself. It's like, when I flirt with you, you just play it through. You don't try to turn it into anything."

I gave her a small smirk. "Shorty, when you flirt with me, it's real obvious that you're... practicing. Like you're testing the waters to see if you've still... *got it* or something."

"Exactly. You let me test the waters without making me feel like you'll expect me to back it up with ass. When I do my little flirty stuff, and you respond, that..."

"Builds your confidence."

"See. Most men aren't like you, Omari. A lot of men wouldn't get that I'm in a weird space, where I need validation from men, but I don't need all the other toxic, messy stuff that comes with it. You're something special. How could I not wonder what dating you would be like?"

"You're something special, too. And I'm sorry that the last nigga you were with didn't recognize or honor that." I paused for a few seconds. "I wanna tell you that you're welcome to practice on me for as long as you want, but I only know how to be real. I can't even say nothing like that, 'cause truth is, I would be mad as hell if you practiced on me then went and gave yourself to the next motherfucker. So, if you wanna practice on me, for a future time when you're ready for me... I'll give you that."

She stared at me silently for a few seconds, before finally speaking. "You just gave me a whole revelation, Mr. Mann. Now I totally get why guys my age like cougars so much. Grown ass energy is just... wow. So, this is grown-man shit, huh?"

"Yep." I nodded slowly. "You like it?"

"I think so. I can definitely appreciate the honesty."

"I'll try to always give you that." I eyed her. "Just match my energy. If you give me honesty, then you give me options on how I want to move. I think that's what liars don't get... hell, or maybe they do. When you lie to people, you take away their option to choose."

"I think people are scared that the other person won't choose them, so they lie."

"Their fear shouldn't give them the right to arbitrarily take away the other person's option to choose."

We fell into silence again. She spent the time taking in the view or soaking up the sun or something. I spent it wondering how much effort and energy I would put into claiming her.

"You know the only thing that would make this place better?" she asked out of the blue.

"What, Kitari?"

"A pool. If you had a pool, you would never be able to get rid of me."

"You've made it obvious that you're obsessed with water. Does Key like to swim?"

She sniggered. "Key is a *total* water baby. She thinks she's a mermaid. I can't get her out of the shower or the bathtub."

"Would you be willing to hang out in Beloit with me?"

"Why? Do you own a home with a pool in Beloit, Wisconsin?" She was suspicious. "Because when we were on my aunt True's dock, you said that you didn't mess with water."

"Let's just say that I know somebody."

She didn't reply right away.

"Would you be open to meeting my mother?" I quickly continued before she could overthink the implications of meeting my parent. "Not on some, '*mom, this is the girl I've been telling you about*,'" I clarified.

She laughed.

"Labor Day is coming up. My moms and her husband typically throw a little something on the grill... and they have a pool. You and Key could roll through with me. Eat. Soak up some sun. Play in the water. Make it a whole thing."

"Let me think about it."

"Cool." Shrugging my shoulders, I added, "No pressure."

"How deep is the pool? I mean, Key loves the water as much as I do, but she doesn't know how to swim yet. She's starting lessons in a few weeks, but for now..."

"She'll be cool. We'll make the necessary adjustments."

"Will your whole family be there?"

"Doubtful. I mean, it's Labor Day. It's not Thanksgiving or Christmas. It'll probably just be my mom, her husband, my siblings, plus you, me, and Key."

"You have siblings? I don't know why, but I thought you were an only child. I don't know. I thought it was you and your mother against the world."

I chuckled lightly. "For the first twenty years of my life, it was. My moms met her husband while I was in high school. He was actually a private fundamentals trainer that she hired for me.

"She worked two-and-a-half jobs to provide for us and to pay dude to come to our house twice a week and work me out. Next thing I know, dude is coming five days a week, and she let go of the part-time job. I mean, I knew what type of time this cat was on when he could hardly get through the workout the first day. Busy burning holes into my mom as she observed. So, when the workouts picked up and the part-time job fell off, I was like, *look at this shit.* When she quit the second job all together and dude was *always* around, I knew it was just a matter of time before he became a more permanent part of my life."

"Do you and this guy not get along?"

"Nah." I chuckled lightly. "Nah, Donald is my guy. I always liked him. But when you're a teenage dude and a man starts hanging around your moms, you automatically assume that he's trying to get the pussy. I didn't want his ass using his access to me, as access to her. But the more I got to know him, the more I was able to see that he was a good guy. He stepped in and took a lot of the financial load off her back. He treats her like a queen. Between him and me, my moms is spoiled as hell. I love that for her because she deserves it. She worked her ass off to make me who and what I am. Everything I am, the man that I am, she gets the credit for that."

"I love the way that you seem to love your mother, not that I would expect anything else," she added quickly. "You seem like a guy who genuinely enjoys women. That's rare these days. I feel like a lot of men don't really enjoy women... at least not as much as they enjoy vaginas."

I couldn't argue with the truth, so I didn't bother trying. She was right, though. I did enjoy women. I enjoyed vagina, as she put it, but I also actually enjoyed women.

"You close with your parents?" I questioned.

"Uh, I'm... I used to be much closer with my mother. I was one of those girls who felt like her mom was her best friend. I told her my secrets, giggled with her... she was my girl. My mother has three daughters, and I was definitely closest to her, until Kinzie came along. She's pretty close to Mom, too. I was never really close to my father. He was..." she took a beat, "he was a chronic gambler. He's in recovery now, but his addiction cost us a lot. We grew up very... transient, always having to move, always having to struggle, even though he had a really good paying job. My mother was always robbing Peter to pay Paul, as she called it. It mostly confused me because, typically, my father was a joyous, happy guy who loved to crack jokes, pull pranks, and love on his girls. But when he was gambling... he wouldn't get belligerent when he fucked up the money, but he would get defiant and dismissive. And my mother would just juggle things and do her best to make everything work out.

"For years I wanted her to divorce him and start over—just the four of us, although it probably would've been the three of us, because Kirbie probably would've stayed with our dad. Anyway, she never did divorce him, which caused me to resent her once I got old enough to understand what was happening."

"Is that why you say that you used to be much closer to her? Because of the way she handled the situation with your father?"

"I think it caused me to lose a certain amount of respect for her. So, when I was in a really bad, really toxic, really damaging relationship, I couldn't... I wouldn't ask for her advice. It was like, how can I listen to you, when you can't even get out of your own messed up situation? We have some residual... mother/daughter stuff that we need to deal with from that period. But instead of dealing with it, we pretend like it never happened or avoid it, which I think keeps us from being as close as we were before." She tilted her head up to the sky for a few seconds. "But one good thing that came out of my relationship with my mom changing was that my relationship with my sister changed. Kirbie and I were never very close growing up."

"Why do you think y'all weren't close?"

"Well, first of all, because she was so different from me. I'm very... girly. Kirbie was always this huge tomboy. She liked to play sports and didn't mind getting dirty or sweaty. She hated shopping. I really couldn't relate to her. Neither could my mother, and she never hid her disdain for Kirbie's preference of being a tomboy.

"As a kid, my mom always harped on the fact that Kirbie was different and 'weird.' That seemed to make it okay for me to label her the same way in my mind. It felt like my mom and I were normal, which made Kirbie... abnormal. Weird. Plus, she acted like our father was super-dad, and that pissed me off. I mean, my mother spent so much time struggling to piece things back together, every time he messed up the money. My mother was working herself to death to keep a roof over our heads and food on the table, and Kirbie acted like our father was the better parent. I couldn't understand it."

The wind shifted, and somewhat cool air rushed across my face. The breeze from the lake felt clean and even a little wet. It offered a refreshing reprieve from the scorching temperatures and stifling humidity that was late summer Chicago.

"It wasn't until I had Key that I realized how wrong my mother was in her treatment of Kirbie." She continued. "A mother's love shouldn't be conditional. More love and acceptance shouldn't be given to one child, or in our case, two children just because they act more like their mother and remind her more of herself. She should've worked harder at accepting and understanding Kirbie.

"My dad let Kirbie be herself, and she knows that he loves her immensely. In the midst of all of his gambling and destroying the fabric of our familial relationships, Kirbie still knew that he loved her. He would always tell our mother that she had Kirbie for him so that he could have a mini-me. Kirbie was his mini-me. And it finally dawned on me. Why would Kirbie twist herself into a pretzel, trying to be what my mother wanted her to be, when it not only made her miserable, but she had my father *right there*, willing and able to accept and love on her just the way she was? I started looking at my younger sister really differently."

I stood and started to gather up our trash. It was mid-afternoon, and even though I would've kept Kitari in my presence late into the night, I knew that eventually, she would need to leave to pick up Key from pre-school.

"When I finally started to climb out of the pit I was in, I needed a job. Kirbie had just gotten hired by Aunt True. She gave me a job as her assistant, even though she didn't need an assistant. I mean, she was an assistant. Anyway, she paid me out of her own pocket for almost a year. She wasn't making any money. Even though True is our aunt, she pays us the market rate. Kirbie's pay was super low. And there she was, literally cashing her check, then depositing it into my account, while she lived off money that Chance gave her. She did that for an entire year. When I asked her why she would do that, she told me, because I'm her sister. After the way I'd treated her growing up, she still looked out for me. Me and Key. Who does that?"

"Apparently, Kirbie."

She snickered. "Yeah, because I can't say that I would've done the same for her."

"But if she needed you today... if you had while she didn't, would you give it to her?"

"In a heartbeat."

I reached my hands to her. When she took them, I helped her stand. Wrapping my arms around her, I bent to whisper in her ear. "That's called growth, mama. Kirbie got there before you, but you still got there."

"I love my sister so much. I hate that she grew up feeling a way and that I contributed to that," she said, her voice cracking. "I would never in a million years do anything to make her doubt herself or feel like I don't love and cherish her. Now, I'm thankful that she's so different from me. She gives me so much balance."

I held her tight to my body and let her work through whatever she needed to work through. Kitari had a lot of shit with her and what seemed to me like deep trauma. She wanted to come out of it, though... and I wanted to support that.

# Six

"And I cried all over his shirt," I admitted to Kirbie as the two of us and our respective daughters sat in the middle of the floor in Chayse's playroom.

"About what?" she probed, snatching Chayse as she walked by to place a flutter of kisses on the toddler's chubby cheek. Chayse shrieked with laughter, as Kirbie repeated the action.

"You're such a good mother to have had such a shitty one," I commented before I caught myself. Slapping a hand over my mouth, I apologized for my language. "Sorry. I meant to think that in my head, not say it out loud."

"Auntie Kit Kat has a potty mouth." Kirbie stage-whispered into her daughter's ear.

"I do. I apologize. But for real. Even though I should've edited my language, the sentiment is spot on. You are a great mom to Chayse, when mom was a really sucky mom to you. How do you do that?"

She shrugged her shoulders. "This will probably sound messed up, but I think of everything—every warm, fuzzy feeling, every positive emotion, every bit of acceptance that I wished I'd gotten from our mother, and I try my hardest to pour that into Chayse."

"That doesn't sound messed up. It sounds like resilience."

We were both quiet for a moment, watching our girls play together.

"What were you crying all over Omari Mann's shirt for?"

"Why you always gotta call him by his whole government name?"

"I don't know." She giggled with a shrug of her slim shoulders. "Anyway, quit trying to deflect. Why were you crying all over his shirt?"

Huffing out a sigh, I worked to compose myself before I answered. "We were talking about family." I sighed again, but this time, more lightly. "He has a really great relationship with his mom. When he asked me about my relationship with mom, I..."

"Started crying?" she filled in for me.

"It hurts that we're not close like we used to be. Mom used to be one of my best friends. Now, she feels like someone that I used to be cool with."

"Do you feel like you'll never get back to where you were with her?" My sister's words were measured, and I was sure that it was because she had her own issues with our mother.

"My feelings are so hurt right now, Kirbs. I feel like she... abandoned me when I needed her the most."

She was almost inaudible. "Same."

Kirbie was right. Our mother had abandoned her for almost her entire life. At least up until the point that Chayse was born. Then she seemed to decide that her middle daughter had accomplished something worth acknowledging. Kirbie was no longer the weird, abnormal daughter in our mother's eyes. I was.

"Right. It's not fair for me to drop this in your lap when she's never been remotely *friendly* toward you."

"She is now, though." She laughed. "We have a similar but opposite problem. You want her attention but don't get it. I get it... and don't want it. Like, I've finally made peace with the idea that the two of us will never have a typical mother/daughter relationship. Now, all of a sudden, she won't get off my phone. It's weird. I feel like she's trying to... slide me into the space that she reserves for you. I don't want that. I don't want to gossip with her or go shopping with her. She knows I hate shopping. She mocked me for the majority of my life about not liking to shop. It's just weird."

"It is weird," I allowed before deciding to change the subject because the current one was getting too heavy. "So, Omari told me that my energy is light and easy. He says he likes it."

"He likes *you*, Kit Kat. Isn't that obvious by now? I mean, even Chance mentioned it."

"Chance mentioned it... when?"

"After Maddox Mayhew's summer camp banquet. Chance said that Omari Mann never took his eyes off of you." She took a beat. "And that Omari looks at you the same way that he looks at me."

I rolled my eyes up to the ceiling. "Chance looks at you with stars in his eyes. He loves your dirty drawers, Kirbie. Omari does not love me."

"Not yet. Just give him a minute."

———

Omari's family held their Labor Day festivities on Sunday as opposed to Monday. So, Key and I rode comfortably—eyes covered by sunglasses—to Beloit, Wisconsin, in his Tesla. His mom texted as we approached her house and asked him to stop and pick up a few bags of ice and two more cases of pop from a local grocery store.

Omari, the gentleman that he was, offered to let Key and me stay in the car, but we were both ready to stretch our legs after driving for almost two hours. So, after putting masks over both Key's mouth and nose, as well as my own, we followed him inside.

The store was crowded, partly because it was a warm Sunday morning, and partly because it was Labor Day weekend. Effortlessly, Omari lifted Key and placed her in the basket of the shopping cart so that we could have our eyes on her at all times.

"Let's do this," he told me as he started to maneuver through the crowd.

It was easy enough to find the soft drink aisle, where he grabbed a case of Sprite and a case of Pepsi. Once Key pointed at the orange pop, he grabbed a case of that, too. I shook my head, because there was no way I would ever purchase an entire case of pop for Key. I totally rationed her soft drink intake, and it would take over a year for her to finish a case. But I let him make it because people who didn't have children tended to overindulge them.

To offset Key's request, I pointed to a twelve-pack of bottled water. Omari gave me a dimpled smirk. "You're right. I should definitely get some water."

"Yes, you should, because that will be what your little friend Key is drinking today."

"Mommy," Key whined.

Omari and I were both focused on Key, so neither of us noticed the woman who had brought her own cart to a complete stop right next to ours.

"O?" she asked.

Omari's head shifted slowly. Not mine. I almost got whiplash looking over at the woman who'd called out to him.

She was a pretty woman, with skin the color of smooth caramel. Dark brown eyes that were round and wide were trained on him. Plump lips and chiseled cheekbones were arranged into a semi-annoyed expression. She was tall, like Kirbie, and slim like her, too. She had a very... model-esque look.

He paid her question in dust, ignoring her and turning the cart completely around in the aisle so that we could head in the opposite direction of the woman.

I didn't say a word. I figured she was somebody from his past since we were in his hometown. If Omari's past was trying to confront him and he didn't want to be bothered... I understood the assignment. Lord only knew how I would react if Elijah tried to confront me in a public place like a grocery store.

"I think that's all we need." He mumbled, barely loud enough for me to hear him.

"So, you finally got the family you always wanted, huh, O?" the feminine voice called out from behind us. "And as big as that baby is, you must've gotten her pregnant before the ink even dried on our divorce papers."

Those words sent a chill up my spine. This woman wasn't some random ex from his youth. This was his ex-wife. And she had fire in her tone.

"She's looking for a fight," I muttered to him as we continued to turn corners with no real destination in mind except... away from old girl.

"She's always looking for a fight. That's her entire mood." He stopped walking. "Take Key back to my car. Let me pay for this stuff and deal with her. I'll meet you outside in a minute."

I was shaking my head before he even got the whole plan out of his mouth. I wasn't leaving him with that chick. Nah. I wasn't leaving him with her. "Nope."

"What do you need, Laila?" he asked the woman, who had closed the distance between us and was now standing right up on our cart, again. "And why are you following me through the grocery store? Didn't you tell the judge that you were afraid of me? Don't you have a restraining order against me? Why are you violating it?"

When Omari told me that he'd had a "hostile" divorce, I didn't imagine restraining orders and such. I was thinking more along the lines of leaked dick pics and obnoxious allegations of infidelity.

"I was afraid of you," she hissed, then elevated her volume. "You threatened me. Does she know that you walked away from our marriage because—"

"I'mma stop you right there." I interrupted her rant, surprising both myself and Omari, because I had no intention of addressing old girl. But she was doing too much. And she was doing it in the grocery store... and in front of my daughter. "Whatever went on in you all's relationship has no bearing on anything this man and I have going on. He's happy now, and apparently, you aren't, but that's not our problem." I looked up at Omari, who was still wearing a frown, and placed my hand gently on his bicep. "Your mom is waiting on us. We should go." I couldn't pretend not to notice that people had their phones out, recording the altercation. I pulled the masks up on both my face and Key's, hoping that neither of us would be identifiable. "We should go, Omari."

Without a word, he started to push the cart toward the check-out line.

We rode the rest of the way to our destination in complete silence. Even Key was quiet, which never happened.

Once we pulled into the driveway of his mom's house, I finally spoke. "Listen, Key is bound to fall asleep on the ride home. We can talk about it... or not talk about it then. I'm about to meet your people for the first time. I have enough anxiety about that; let's not add anymore. Okay?"

"Yeah," he said shortly. "I'm good with that."

Omari's mother answered the door for us, with a huge friendly smile on her face.

"My one and only," she said, before motioning with her hands so he would know to bend down and hug her.

She embraced him tightly, seemingly holding on for dear life. He stayed bent, allowing her to hug him for as long as she needed—not releasing her until she released him first. Before she did so, she kissed his bearded cheek, then wiped her lipstick from it.

"You know you have two other children now, right? You can't keep referring to me as your *one and only*. You're gonna make them feel some type of way." He teased her.

"You were my one and only for twenty years. If they can't handle that, then I don't know what to tell them."

I chuckled at her response, which drew her attention to me.

She gave me the once-over. "Hello, gorgeous."

"Hello," I said, shyly.

"I'm not gonna embarrass my son and make a fuss over you just because he hasn't brought a girl home for me to meet in... years. I'll just say that I'm Amina. Please, call me Mina."

"I'm Kitari. This is my daughter; we call her Key. It's nice to meet you."

"Well, aren't you pretty?" Mina addressed Key. "How old are you, sugar?"

"Four," Key replied, holding up fingers to solidify her answer.

"I remember when my kids were four. That's such a fun age. Let me see if you like the same kinds of things that my kids liked when they were four years old." She pretended to think. "Do you like to color?"

Key nodded enthusiastically. "I like to color with my purple marker. It's my favorite."

"Well, purple is the color of royalty, so you must be a princess."

"My mommy says that."

"Your mommy is right. Do you like to... blow bubbles?"

"Yes. I love bubbles."

"Okay. Okay. It seems like you and I might be able to have some fun together," Mina said. "But I have to see how you answer this final question, Miss Key. Do you like... swimming pools?"

Key's eyes could have bugged right out of her sockets. "I love swimming pools."

Mina clapped her hands in excitement. "I love that! Your mommy's friend, Omari, had my husband prepare an entire swimming pool just for you, because our pool is too deep to be safe. Would you like to see the one we prepared for you?"

"Yes! Yes! Yes!" Key jumped up and down. "I have on my swimming suit under my dress, Miss Mina."

"So, you're all ready to dive in?"

"Actually, it was a long ride here, Mina. Can I take her to the bathroom first?" I asked.

"Of course, you can. I'll wait for you to get ready, Miss Key, then we will go see this swimming pool."

"Yay!" Key celebrated, and I couldn't help smiling at how joyful she was about the prospect of a swimming pool.

The pool that Omari had his stepfather prepare for Key was inflatable and shallow, but that didn't make the extra-large structure any less impressive. Key floated, splashed around, pretended to swim, pretended to be a mermaid, and generally just lived her best life in that pool for over three hours. When she was finally ready to get out, her skin was beyond puckered.

Omari's younger siblings were both teenagers. His brother was sixteen, and his sister was fourteen, so they stayed just long enough to meet Key and me and offer polite conversation, before they left to hang with their own friends.

Omari's mother and stepfather kept us entertained, and Key was the star of their show. Although Mina didn't drop any hints about being ready for grandchildren from Omari, she didn't need to. It was obvious by the way she catered to and showered Key with attention. And Donald wasn't much better. He let Key bully him into counting to one hundred no less than twenty-five times. It was Omari who finally told her to let Donald make it. Then, she coaxed him into picking up where Donald left off.

Late in the afternoon, after we'd eaten and communed, Omari decided that we needed to get on the road. Mina invited Key and me into the kitchen so that she could pack up some to-go plates for us.

I set Key at the kitchen island and handed her my cell phone so she could watch educational videos while Mina and I worked.

"Listen," Mina began after glancing quickly at Key to make sure she was pretty much engrossed in her show. "I sat in that backyard and heard both you and my son express over and over that you all are only friends. And I can accept that. All I want to say is that Omari seems happy." She sighed lightly. "Omari... these last few years have been challenging for my big baby. That's what I call him—my big baby because he was taller than me by the time he was twelve, but he was still my baby.

"The challenges have made him a little bit of a commitment-phobe. It's almost to the point where he wants to reject teams... and sometimes people, before they get a chance to reject him. He refuses to settle down in any city... won't buy a house... won't invest in the community. Treats every team and every city like a temporary visit. When he told me he made an offer on a place, I was... shocked. He hasn't bought a property in... at least five years. I wondered what made him buy something in Chicago, especially since I know how much he hates the Midwest.

"Donald said that he'd bet there was a woman behind Omari's sudden change of heart, but I wasn't so sure. Then, he shows up with you and that pretty, precious little princess of yours, and it has me wondering."

I chuckled at her lack of subtlety. "I'll take some of the credit for convincing him." I acceded. "But only because I kinda poured it on thick about how much of a great investment a property with a view of the lake is in Chicago. I mean, even if he moves on after one year with the Bison, he's still gonna make a profit on the sale of the place."

"Tuh." She sucked her teeth. "Omari doesn't care about that kind of stuff. I mean, he cares about making money, but he wouldn't buy a property for the money-making possibilities, especially not in this area."

"I did tell him that I loved the place. And that if I had the money, I would buy it for myself and Key," I finally admitted.

"Ooooookay." She chortled. "Now the truth comes out."

I laughed along with her.

"So, Donald was absolutely right. You influenced my son to buy a home in Chicago." She glanced over at me appreciatively. "I'm thankful. This gives me hope that my son might be coming out of this funk. He might actually *try* this time. He might actually try to make a place for himself on the Bison."

"I hope so," I told her earnestly. "I think Omari has good seasons left in him. He thinks he's winding down, but I don't think he's tapped all of the potential that he has inside of him. I think there are definitely things that he'll bring to the Bison."

She didn't respond, beyond a knowing smirk, as she wrapped several heavily filled plates with aluminum foil. She cut her eyes at my daughter. "Is that your best friend?"

"Most of the time," I confessed with a small smile playing on my lips. "She's the thing that keeps me pushing, even..."

"When you want to give up?" Mina finished for me. "She's your ride or die?"

I practically guffawed. "More like, I'm her ride or die. She doesn't even realize the lengths and the depths I would go to just to keep her happy and safe. I would sacrifice me... I have sacrificed me." The last statement came out without my permission. I wanted to bite it back because it was too telling. It was from too deep down inside of me.

"You're preaching to the choir," she mumbled. "Has Omari told you anything about our relationship?"

I nodded, afraid to speak, because I didn't want any more bones from the skeletons in my closets to come flying out of my mouth.

"I had Omari when I was sixteen years old... and a young sixteen at that. I was the epitome of a baby raising a baby. Luckily, my family was supportive because Omari's father was... not. My family was supportive but generally 'hands-off.' They let me do my thing and make basically all of the decisions regarding him. Looking back, I wish they would've spoken up more, especially when they saw me making missteps. Luckily, I was a quick study, and I don't think my shortcomings had too many long-term effects on my son. But when I tell you we grew up together... baaaabyyyy. Omari and I might as well have sat next to each other in kindergarten."

We both laughed heartily.

"I sense a sadness in your spirit, Kitari." She finished placing the plates of food into a plastic grocery bag and took both of my hands in hers. "You have a lightness about you... but it is bogged down by this gray rain cloud that I see hanging over your head."

My eyes started to well with tears.

"Whatever is weighing on you... bringing you down... if my son is the cure, the antidote for that, let him be that. Open your heart and mind and let him give you that. And I don't necessarily mean that in the romantic sense. I mean, if he's a good friend who comes around and makes you laugh or lightens your load, let him do that. Don't deny yourself those moments. Single motherhood can be a draining, difficult, lonely beast. Grab your joy where you can. Okay?"

I nodded, tears now coursing down my face.

"Look at me, acting like I'm your mother." Quickly, she swiped two paper towels from the holder and handed them to me. "Your own mother has probably..."

I shook my head and cut her off. "My mother can't relate to my situation," I said through light sniffles while dabbing at my leaky eyes.

She pulled me into a hug that seemed almost as tight as the one she'd given Omari upon our arrival. "Single motherhood is a sorority that pledges you hard as hell. You get accepted on-line, and the hazing begins right away."

I chuckled at her analogy.

"Am I lying?" she questioned, chuckling herself, as she released me.

I shook my head. I'd never pledged a sorority, but I'd heard stories.

"And when you cross those burning sands and get the letters M.O.M. branded on you... girl. That's when the real work begins." She released me. "If you don't hear it enough, Kitari, you're doing a fabulous job with your daughter. She's lovely. She's polite. She's inquisitive. She's bright. She's absolutely stunning. That one's energy is huge. She was a joy to be around today. Thank you for bringing her. I would say that she gives me *baby fever*, but this factory is closed. I'll say that she gives me grandbaby fever. I'm about to start hounding Omari right now about bringing me some grandchildren home to spoil, and he has you to thank for that," she jested.

"Oh no."

"Yep," she stated with a vigorous head nod. "Yes, ma'am. Either that, or you need to agree to bringing Key out here to spend time with Donald and me."

"Ain't nobody agreeing to make this two-hour drive every time you want to see Key. You need to get Kitari's number and connect with Key over FaceTime or something." Omari joined us in the kitchen. "What've y'all been doing in here all this time? Yakking?"

"Don't worry about it," Mina responded, hands on her well-defined hips. "Stay outta women's business."

"Whatever." He waved her off. "You got the food ready or what, Shirley?"

Chuckling lightly, she punched him ineffectually in the bicep. "I've got your Shirley, boy."

She went to punch him again, but he caught her wrist, brought her fist to his mouth, and kissed it. I watched her very obviously melt with love for her son.

"That boy can't do no wrong in his momma's eyes," Donald staged-whispered to me.

"Don't be a hater all your life," Omari chided, pulling his mother into his arms, practically lifting her off of her feet. "She was mine first."

"Now she's mine... in a completely different way," Donald responded.

"I'm both of yours," she clarified, as she and Omari ended their hug. "Actually, I'm all four of yours."

"Again, you were mine first," Omari reiterated.

"You're right, spoiled brat. Is that what you want to hear?" Amina reached up and brushed more errant lipstick from his cheek.

"Yep." He ran his hand over her neatly coiffed hair, mussing it.

"Boy!" She popped his large hand with her much smaller one.

"Come on, Mina."

"Mina?" She popped him again.

Donald turned his attention to me. "This is what I have to put up with when he comes to visit. They act like siblings." He shook his head in mock pity, but the smirk on his face let me know that he enjoyed their banter.

Omari shook Donald's hand before pulling him into a quick embrace. "Take care, man."

"You, too. Be safe driving back," Donald offered.

"Ay, pretty lady, grab the plates, while I grab the luggage," Omari told me, then scooped Key into his strong arms.

She giggled happily. "I'm not luggage, Mari. I'm a girl."

"Oh yeah? I thought you were my suitcase," he teased, heading toward the front door.

I grabbed the bag filled with food and brought up the rear.

———

We had barely made it a mile from Amina and Donald's house before Key's light snoring could be heard from the back seat.

Omari cleared his throat. "Ay, thanks for what you did at the grocery store. That whole situation's been playing in the back of my mind almost all day. And if you wouldn't have gotten me out of there... things coulda went really bad. Thanks for keeping a calm head..." He trailed off.

I waved him off. "No worries. I don't know how I would feel if I unexpectedly ran into my ex in a public setting, so... there's that. It just seemed like it was best if we got out of there. I mean, she was looking for a fight, and she was doing all her... *the most* in front of a crowd and in front of Key. There was no way for things to end well. I just wanted all three of us to get out of there."

He sighed but kept driving in silence.

"You know we have like, two hours in the car. You can tell me your story, if you want. If you need to talk... to get it out, I'm here. I'll listen." I paused thoughtfully before adding, "I should preface that invitation by saying that my own last relationship was a shit show that crashed and burned. So, I don't have any good advice, pearls of wisdom, or gems to drop. But I will listen."

He still didn't speak, but I got the distinct impression that he would... in time. Instead, I filled in the silence.

"Are both of you from Beloit? You and your ex? Were you high school sweethearts or something?"

"We're both from the area. She's not from Beloit, but she's from the area. I didn't meet her until I was in the league. I was in my seventh year... on my third team, St. Louis. I met her at a benefit for The Boys & Girls Club of Greater Northern Wisconsin. She worked for the Wisconsin Tourism Board, and I... I'm from the community, and I spent some time at The Boys & Girls Club as a kid. So I was there as the keynote speaker and as a donor.

"Anyway, I was introduced to Laila, and she was just... she was like my young boy fantasy in real life—the beautiful small-town girl who had an air of sophistication and cosmopolitan appeal about her, but who also wanted the white picket fence outside of the public eye. Up until Laila, I'd spent my time dating and fucking chicks with that real *slick*, manufactured look. You know... big ass, miniscule waist, fat thighs, hair always in a perfect ass-touching ponytail or the perfectly *beach-waved* sew-in—women who understood which one of their sides was the best to be photographed on.

"Those women had a place. They were good as hell for optics. When you wanted to make your socials blow up or you wanted to flex, you just posted a picture of yourself with one of those women on your arm. Niggas envied your ability to pull the picture-perfect chick. But in my mind, those weren't the types of women I wanted to settle down with... They were for playing. When Laila showed up, I felt like I found the image that had been in my head all along."

"Was it love at first sight?" I teased.

"Shit, it was something. We met in June and got married in February."

"Wow."

"Yeah, wow. It was... intense. It felt like Laila brought out the best in me. I played my best basketball while I was with her. My numbers were crazy... got voted to the All-Star Game for the first time in my career. Home was good. Career was good. Everything was good."

"Must've been a great time to be Omari Mann," I joked.

He chuckled. "It was definitely a great time to be me. My life was better than it had ever been. Laila was this... force, and I just loved the shit out of that girl. She was my own personal angel. She'd been in a major life-threatening accident a few years before I met her. She'd been on the back of a motorcycle with her boyfriend when it crashed. According to Laila and her family, the accident was life-altering for both her and dude who was driving the motorcycle. Multiple broken bones, multiple contusions, multiple surgeries.

"Somehow, the motorcycle ended up coming down on top of both of them. Broke dude's back, messed up his spine, and left him in a wheelchair. Laila fared better, but she was still messed up. Just hearing about her being in an accident of that magnitude made me even more protective over her than I would have naturally been, especially because the trauma of the accident caused her so much mental grief. She spent a lot of time in therapy, dealing with the aftermath of almost losing her life like that.

"When I met her, she'd just actually gotten back from what she called her 'year of me.' She'd traveled across Europe with her sister, doing all of the things she was scared to do before the accident."

"That must've been empowering. Good for her, for facing her fear like that. If only we could all be so bold and not need a near death experience to jumpstart it. Good for her."

"Yeah." He agreed, noncommittal.

An easy silence settled over the truck as we drove. Just as the light strains of Jay-Z could be heard floating from the stereo, Omari started to speak again.

"After we'd been married for two years—she was four, almost five years out from her accident—we felt pretty solid in what we had. We started to discuss having a family. She was from a family with three kids. You know that I basically grew up as an only child. We both wanted kids... in theory. We'd talked about it, and it wasn't a deal breaker, but we were gonna try. My only caveat was that if we had a kid, we needed to have more than one. Being an only child... I didn't want that for my kid."

He let a few beats pass before he spoke into the silence again. "We had a gathering for our third wedding anniversary. We'd eloped. Just flew Amina, Donald, my siblings, her siblings, and her parents to Miami one weekend during the season and did it. Got married on the beach with like ten people in attendance. So, we'd never had any kind of big party to celebrate our union.

"Year three, we decided that we would do that. We waited until the season was over, rented a big house in the Hamptons, had the whole shit decked out, and threw this huge party. We met each other's families, and it was just a good time... until it wasn't."

"Oh, no. What happened?" My stomach sank at the thought that his relationship went bad at his anniversary party.

"We're all standing around in a group talking, laughing, shooting the shit. Some random ass uncle of hers had brought his girlfriend along for the festivities. She starts talking to Laila. Tells her that we're a beautiful couple and starts talking about how cute our kids are gonna be. Then she flat out asks Laila when she's gonna give me babies. Before Laila can compose herself, the uncle speaks up and literally says, 'See, I told you that you talk too much. Laila can't give him babies. All her shit got crushed in a motorcycle accident when she was younger. Only way she having babies is buying 'em or stealing 'em.'" He said the last part as a joke, but who jokes about something like that? A loud ass fucking hush came over the crowd."

"Oh, no," I repeated.

"So many thoughts went through my mind in like the matter of a millisecond. My life changed the second those words left her uncle's mouth. To find out something like that—something as delicate as that, in a space filled with strangers—was some bullshit."

"You don't have to describe your feelings to me," I assured him. "My life was blown up in front of a group of strangers, too. Then blown up a second time on social media."

"Say less. I'm familiar with that, too, because my shit got blown up for a second time on social media as well."

"What happened after the uncle dropped the bomb?" I probed, my curiosity getting the best of me.

"I actually played it through. I pulled Laila into my arms and assured the watching crowd that we were currently discussing our options and that her health and wellness were our main concerns. I smiled and joked my way through that entire anniversary celebration, knowing that my marriage was over."

I let a few moments pass before I felt compelled to ask the question burning in my mind. "I thought kids weren't a dealbreaker. What made you feel like your marriage was over, when you were okay with not having kids?"

"I didn't like feeling manipulated... or lied to... or hell, made a fool of. The deception. When she decided she would withhold the truth from me, she left it open for me to hear the truth from somebody else. That wasn't what marriage looked like to me. For me, marriage is protecting one another from harm, from hurt, from embarrassment, from unnecessary scrutiny. I would've protected Laila with my life. I shared myself with her fully. Had no idea that she wasn't matching that energy. Had to hear it from Uncle Sherrod.

"Then, once the shit hit the fan and she realized that she couldn't manipulate me into staying in the marriage, she took her fight to social media to try me in the court of public opinion. She made the case that I left her because she couldn't have my children, leaving out the fact that she never told me that she couldn't carry children. And that was completely unfair."

"Even if it was true, her taking it to social media was messed up. It's never cool when an ex drags you on the internet."

"Say less," he mumbled.

# SEVEN

OMARI

By the time I pulled to a stop in front of Kitari's building, both she and Key were asleep. Kitari, however, opened her eyes when the car cut off.

"Did I fall asleep on you?" Her voice sounded surprised.

"Yeah, you did. It's cool, though. It gave me a minute to sort out my thoughts." I grabbed the car keys from where they sat inside the cup holder. "I got Key. You just bring yourself."

When we got into her unit, I followed as she directed me to Key's bedroom. It was decorated sparsely, but everything a child would need was there—bed, dresser, chest of drawers, nightstand. Kitari rummaged around in one of the drawers, while I removed the sandals from Key's feet.

When Kitari produced pajamas, that was my cue to leave the room.

"You can wait for me in the living room," she told me. "I just need to get her undressed, and I'll be right there."

A few minutes later, Kitari entered the living room. "Hey. Thanks for everything today, Omari. That pool you had your stepdad set up was... everything. Key had a ball, and I did, too. Your mom is really nice. Hanging out with her made me miss having that relationship with my own mom, but not in a way that hurt or anything. It was nice. She's really nice."

"Mina is crazy as hell, but she's cool as hell, too."

Nodding her agreement, she sat down next to me on the sofa, then placed her right hand on my knee. "Don't feel like you have to get right back on the road. That was a long drive. If you need to chill for a minute, or you want something to eat..."

"Just ask for what you want, Kitari," I told her before adding. "You already know I'mma give it to you."

"Okay." She chuckled lightly. "You know I like spending time with you. I'm not ready for you to leave, yet."

I cut my gaze up to the ceiling. "The shit you say."

"What?" she asked, feigning innocence. She gave up the ruse when she spoke again. "I don't know, Omari. You make me... bold. You make me feel like I don't have to edit myself with you."

"Do you often feel like you have to edit yourself?"

She seemed to consider the question. "I had a hard time determining what people wanted from me in the past. I think that might be a hall-mark of children with parents who have addictions. My dad was so... complicated. I really couldn't figure him out. I just knew that we, our family, wasn't enough for him. We weren't enough to keep him away from the casino or the boat or the bingo hall or the football pool, or any of the other ways he gambled his paycheck away. And based on her rela-tionship with Kirbie, my mother always made it clear that her love and acceptance were conditional. I got it because I was like her. So, I very rarely did anything I didn't think she would approve of."

"Yeah." I nodded because I could understand her point.

"Anyway, you have this demeanor where you act like... or maybe I just assume that you'll take me however I give myself to you... on some friendship stuff, Omari. I don't mean in a romantic relationship or anything like that. I feel like you'll be my friend... We'll stay cool if I'm my organic self around you," she took a very deep breath, "which is really good because I'm still trying to figure myself out. I don't really know who I am yet."

"I think figuring yourself out is lifelong work, mama."

"Yeah." She nodded her agreement. "I'm trying to be intentional about applying the lessons I've learned from my fuckups in the past. You know, so I can grow from them."

Another nod from me.

"So, your ex-wife lying by omission killed the marriage for you?" she asked.

What exactly killed my marriage was a question I'd gone around and around with before, during, and even after my divorce.

"Yooooo," I dragged the word out. "It wasn't the fact that she couldn't give me children. She likes to pretend like that was it. Other people think that was the reason. I've even debated with myself about if that was really the reason, and it wasn't.

"Blaming it on the lying by omission would be more accurate. When it comes down to it, it wasn't necessarily the lying, either. It was what the lying represented. The fact that it was a trigger that I didn't even realize was a trigger until I was in that situation.

"When she wasn't upfront with me about her medical history and let me marry her anyway... she took away my choice. She took away my option to choose her over the fact that she couldn't birth children, because let's be real. Just because she couldn't carry or conceive children doesn't mean we couldn't have them. There's always adoption or fostering... surrogacy. I'm saying, a home girl of mine put herself through college doing egg donations. We could've bought some damn eggs."

"You *are* in the NBA." She co-signed. "It's not like you couldn't afford it."

"But Laila didn't give us the chance to have those discussions. She made the unilateral decision that I would go into the marriage without the knowledge, and I would just have to what? Deal with it?

"That was when I realized that people taking my options, making decisions for me, on my behalf, without my consent, is a trigger for me. Every time I thought about the fact that there were people out there who knew more about the woman that I slept next to at night, more about the state of my marriage than I did... it bugged the hell outta me. But when I thought about the fact that she let me commit my life to hers without all of the information to truly make that decision soundly... it gave me fucking heart palpitations.

"Have your secrets. If you went by the frat house and fucked everybody in there on a dare from your college roommate when you were nineteen, you ain't gotta tell me that. But something like you can't physically carry children or you have a terminal illness or you were born as the opposite gender that you now present as... tell me that! Give me the facts. Let me decide. Because I still would've chosen Laila. If she would've given me the chance... I would've chosen her."

"Does she know that? Did she know that then?"

"Yeah, I told her. I told her that if she had kept it trill in the beginning, I would've rocked with her. If kids weren't in our future... so be it. But the underhanded shit that she pulled... the dumb ass shit that she pulled? Nah, ain't no way to really come back from that. How you gon' keep a secret from your husband that your entire family knows? It was bound to come out at some point... and it did. Had we had an actual wedding, it probably would've come out then. Some well-meaning relative of hers would've gotten drunk and said some stupid shit about not believing that I would marry her, knowing she couldn't have kids. There was no way for it not to come out. I was low key a little pissed with myself for marrying somebody who was dumb enough to think that it wouldn't come out."

When she started to guffaw, I couldn't help but to chuckle with her.

"I'm starting to get hungry," Kitari said once she'd composed herself. "You think we should grab a couple of those plates from the car?"

"You still ain't ready for me to go?" I teased her.

She shook her head but didn't speak. I didn't push her.

After watching her for a few moments, I spoke. "I got you." She was so damn pretty as it was. And with that look of need in her eyes, there was absolutely no way that I could deny her. And that was a problem for me.

At my car, I grabbed the food and one of several gym bags that I kept in the trunk. I had anywhere from two to three in there at any given time, because I never knew when I would feel the urge to hit up the gym for a workout or when I might get a call from Gideon out the blue.

Kitari stood back and let me walk into her condo upon my return.

"Ay," I called out to her, as she led me to where I could drop the food on the peninsula that separated her kitchen from her dining space and living room. "Do you mind if I take a shower? I'm sweaty as hell, and I smell like smoke from the grill from messing around with Donald and my mother."

"Same." She agreed. "Uh, you can shower in the hallway bathroom. Let me grab you a towel and some soap and... stuff."

She was doing that thing where she eye-fucked me again.

"Yo, stop eye-fucking me, Kitari. You can shower with me if you want to. I'm getting the distinct impression that you wanna see me naked. See if the big dick energy is just a stunt, or if I'm really holding." Once I started messing with her, I couldn't seem to stop. "I told you to ask for whatever you want, and I'mma give it to you."

"That shower's not big enough for two people."

I loved the way that she held her own and didn't back down from me.

"Well, we should grab Key, the food, and whatever else you need and head to my place. 'Cause my shower's big as shit."

She eyed me thoughtfully. "Next time..." she paused, "but for now, you can shower in my bathroom... with me."

I figured she wasn't lying when she said that I made her bold, because a few weeks ago, she never would've said anything like that to me.

She turned and headed in the direction that I presumed her bedroom was in, not bothering to check to see if I was following her, which, of course, I was.

Her master bathroom seemed to be one of the larger rooms in her small condo. The room was a nice size, big enough for her to have a separate shower and tub. I pulled my T-shirt over my head, placed it on the vanity, then flipped the toilet seat up and took a much-needed piss.

"Be right back," she told me. "I have to pee, and even though I want to be bold enough to just pee right here in front of you... I'm not that bold. I'll be right back."

I watched her go with a chuckle. In two seconds flat, I was naked, fiddling around with the knobs, trying to adjust the water. I heard her reenter the room, but I didn't turn around. "Should I set the water on 'hell?' I know women like for it to be scalding."

"I don't know. If I get cold, are you gonna warm me up?"

"Stop practicing your flirty shit on me, Kitari, and get over here."

As she walked closer to me, I turned my attention from the knobs and gave it to her. Naked Kitari was my favorite sight to date. Her chocolate-covered skin was smooth and flawless. She wasn't a slim woman—she actually wasn't even slim—thick—but she wasn't full-figured, either. She was thick as fuck in all the right places, not a measurement out of proportion. Her waist to hips ratio wasn't manufactured. She was perfection from the roundness of her arms and stomach to the plumpness of her tear-drop titties, from her ebony areolas with taunt nipples standing at attention to the curviness of her thighs and ass. Every inch of her body was exactly what her clothes made me imagine it would be.

"Damn, you know you're gorgeous, right? You know you're the baddest motherfucker walking, right?" I took her in with absolutely no shame that my eyes rested exactly where they wanted to rest for as long as they wanted to rest there. When my eyes finally made their way to her face, she was blushing. "Come here."

She walked over to me slowly as hell, and the anticipation made my heart rate speed up and my dick start to swell. When she was close enough, I pulled her into my arms and held her to me. "Is this what you need, baby? Somebody to hold you? Somebody to love up on you without necessarily fucking up on you?"

She wrapped her arms around my waist and buried her face in my upper ab area. Even though she didn't respond to my questions, the way she was holding onto me told me that she needed to be held.

I never understood or even thought about how important touch and intimacy could be to women, until Donald came into my life. I was seventeen years old, and thought I was a man. Then he came along and showed me that I had a lot to learn, and that I wasn't too old to need a father—or at least a father figure—in my life. All it took was for me to come at him wrong about his dealings with my mother for him to teach me a lesson about life.

Donald didn't sit me down and have a heart to heart with seventeen-year-old me. Instead, he made me bust my ass in a workout, while he dropped gems right into my lap. He was breezy but firm with me about what my mother needed as a woman. About how even though her relationship with her son was satisfying in many ways, in other ways, it put her at a deficit. He talked about the parts of her that went unnurtured and unfed because she was dedicated to pouring into me; how she was feeding me while she starved. Then he told me that he wanted the job of feeding her. Although football had never been my game, I quickly tackled his ass in the grass. I didn't want any dude talking to me about "feeding" my mother, and definitely not when all I could think of was him wanting to feed her dick until he met the next athlete's mother that he could feed dick to.

Donald let me get some of my anger off, then he pinned me to the ground. That only served to piss me off even more, and I swore that when he let me up, I was gonna kill his ass. But then he started talking to me about feeding my mother's soul, making her see herself as a beautiful, vibrant young woman with an existence outside of mother to her son. Because the truth of the matter was that I was headed off to college, and her job raising me would essentially be done.

Kitari needed to know that there was more to her than just "mother of Key." She was still a beautiful, vibrant young woman. She was hungry. I wanted nothing more than to feed her.

After carrying her into the shower stall, I proceeded to douse her sponge with her shower gel of choice. I washed her gently and thoroughly, cleansing every part of her body twice as she stood there like a statue with her eyes squeezed shut and let me.

Once I had her fully soaped, I spoke. "Rinse off, Kitari." She moved under the stream of water, while I quickly washed myself with her sponge.

After the shower, she looked into my eyes. "I'm exhausted, Omari. I don't know if it was spending the day in the sun... or what. All I know is that I need sleep." That was followed by a large yawn, after which she added, "but don't go."

"You want me to watch you sleep?" I questioned jokingly as I ran the towel over my body, picking up the last few water droplets.

She was watching my dick too hard to respond at first.

"My eyes are up here, lil mama. And you ain't too sleepy to watch my dick, huh?"

Her neck snapped, and her head flew up with her eyes crashing into mine. "Sorry. Sorry. What were you saying?"

A short chuckle accompanied my head shake. "I ain't fucking wit' you, Kitari."

She gave me a lazy, sleepy grin. "You have a nice body, Omari. I'm tired," she repeated. "You're gonna have to let me make it on the fact that I was staring. And no, I don't want you to watch me sleep, smart ass. I want you to hold me. Your arms feel good wrapped around me."

"You feel good wrapped up in my arms, shorty." I dropped the towel.

"Please, put some clothes on."

"You first, because I swear on everything, it's taking every bit of will power I have not to fuck you right now."

She let her eyes move over my body one last time. "Same." Then she practically ran over to her closet and closed herself inside.

I cupped my balls gently, because Kitari was gonna have them blue as hell.

A few minutes later, the two of us were stretched out in her bed. We were bathed in the warm orange-ish glow streaming through her sheer curtains from the streetlight that sat right outside her window. Originally, I'd been lying there thinking that I needed to buy baby girl some black-out curtains for her bedroom, but the sheer curtains let in light... which allowed me to see her. Once again, I wasn't ashamed that I let my eyes eat her up.

She was wearing a T-shirt and panties. I was wearing basketball shorts and socks. We were on our sides, facing one another. Her face was nestled in my chest, while my hand methodically moved through her ponytail. The rhythmic beating of her heart was starting to lull me to sleep, when her voice cut through the stillness.

"I honestly can't remember the last time I was this horny."

I laughed heartily, from deep in my gut. "Yo, say less," I told her through the guffaws. "I'm telling you, I was laying here feeling like I was on some simp shit, because my dick is hard as hell from just the smell of you."

"I'm trying so hard to fall asleep," she admitted. "But sleep will not come."

"I was almost there before you started talking," I shared.

"Sorry."

"You're straight," I assured her. After a few beats of silence, I spoke again. "Let me help you relieve some tension." I moved my hand between her legs, loving that she spread them for me. My hand dipped inside her panties and quickly found her swollen bud.

"Uuuuhhhhhmmm." She moaned for me, grinding into my finger. "You should let me relieve your tension, too."

"How you gonna do that?" I drew lazy circles around and over her clit, sometimes allowing my finger to slip just barely inside her opening.

"Take off your shorts and drawers, and I'll show you," she promised on a hum of pleasure.

It took me all of two seconds to divest myself of the little bit of clothing I was wearing, while she did the same. Once we were both naked again, she climbed on top of me, her legs spread even wider than they were before. I didn't ask any questions; I just put my hands on her waist and pulled her little ass up my body until her pussy was on my lips. She adjusted quickly and was able to swipe her tongue over the head of my dick, capturing the pre-cum, right before I let my own tongue swipe her clit.

She must've liked the taste of my pre-cum, because she was giving the head of my dick all types of love, making me an even bigger fan of hers than I already was.

"Shit, Kitari." When she bobbed her head and encapsulated my entire dick in the warm, moist wetness of her mouth, my eyes rolled back in my head. Using a suck/lick/spit/slurp method, she had me fighting back moans, completely distracting me from focusing on giving her reciprocity.

I dug my fingers into her thighs, making indentations in her supple flesh.

She hummed while happily deep throating me. I returned the favor by attempting to devour her pussy. An orgasm found her first, bringing vibrations, uncontrollable shaking, and groans from low in her throat. As soon as she came back to earth, she clamped her lips back around my dick, letting saliva saturate me. She pumped and sucked, picking up speed, and gagging. She gobbled me up until her reward shot down her throat.

———

"Shit!"

That one word, spoken in the tone and at the volume that it was spoken, pulled me from a deep slumber. After a few involuntary blinks, I was able to open my eyes enough to find Kitari sitting on the edge of the bed. It was weird because I distinctly remembered falling asleep with her planted firmly on top of me. Now, she was sitting up, her phone in hand, a frown on her face. I rolled over and wrapped my arm around her waist as well as I could.

"What's up?" I probed, my face resting in the curve of her back.

She relaxed into me slightly, but I could still feel the tension in her spine. She sighed.

"What's up, gorgeous? What has you frowning like that?"

She handed me her phone without looking at me. "My aunt True has a hard time sleeping at night. She uses that time to scroll through social media to make sure there's nothing incriminating or potentially damaging about any of her clients popping up. She found that."

I looked down at the phone. It was a TikTok. Elijah Emerson's account.

*When your hoe ass ex has the next nigga acting like he's the daddy.*

That was the caption under a video. I could see without even pushing the little arrow that it was the scene that played out in the grocery store earlier in the day. I tapped the arrow and heard Kitari say, "Your mom is waiting on us. We should go."

Another video from Elijah followed the first one.

*What the fuck kinda lame ass nigga introduces Kitty Yum-Yum to his moms? The fuck wrong with this motherfucka? I was fucking her for two years; she ain't never even met my second cousin, let alone moms.*

There were "likes," and comments for days under the video. Even though I tried not to notice, I did.

*I wondered whatever happened to her.* Read the first one.

*You had a baby wit' Kitty Yum-Yum????? Nigga, strap up!!!*

*I see she found a new professional athlete's dick to bounce up and down on.* Read another.

*You dodged a bullet with that bitch, Double E. Mariah Freeman-Emerson is a HUGE come up from Kitty Yum-Yum's heaux ass.*

*With receipts like these, she making it extra easy for me to get full custody of daddy's little girl.*

"So, Elijah Emerson is Key's dad?" I asked, setting the phone down on the bed.

"He is *not* her father. He apparently *thinks* he's her father. He's on social media *claiming* to be her father."

I took a different route. "What do you claim him to be?"

"The asshole who tried to wreck me. The first dude to break me... but not destroy me."

"He's asking for full custody of Key?"

"He's threatening to sue for full custody. He'll never get it."

She sounded confident, even though her posture was anything but.

"You sure about that?"

She finally turned around on the bed and faced me full on. "What judge would give him custody of a child that is not biologically his?"

"Y'all had a paternity test done?"

"I don't need a paternity test. Key is not his."

"If he sues you for custody, you know the judge is more than likely going to require that you do a paternity test, even if it's to rule him out."

"Yeah." She nodded. "That's why I have Kirbie working on getting an injunction. I'm doing everything I can to keep him from getting that test."

I felt like the two of us were talking in circles, so I decided to switch subjects. "Who is Kitty Yum-Yum?"

She sighed again before pushing her messy hair out of her face. After a few moments of silence, Kitari told me a story about a high school graduate who had no desire to attend college but was sent there anyway by her well-meaning mother.

"My mother had no business sending me away to college, when she knew our family didn't have the money to support me. I mean, most every college student is broke as hell, but I was a special kind of broke. What extra money did my mother have when she was constantly trying to fill in the gaps my father was making with his gambling? Plus, she had two daughters still at home that required financial attention. If I got twenty dollars from her every two weeks, it was a good two weeks."

*Dayum*, I thought to myself but kept quiet.

"While I was at school, I watched this documentary on Netflix or something about some white chick who had put herself through college by doing porn. I knew that wasn't for me. There were a lot of chicks on campus who were stripping at night. I didn't have the balls to prance around anybody's stage butt ass naked. I did have the balls to start my own *Only For Fans* account, though. Kitty Yum-Yum was my alter-ego."

"For thirty-nine ninety-nine a month, people could see what? You playing with your own pussy? What?"

"For nineteen ninety-nine a month, my subscribers could watch me model itty bitty swimsuits, lingerie, thongs, five- and six-inch hooker heels. I didn't play with myself or do anything overtly sexual, but everything I did was done with... gratuitous flirtiness.

"I modeled my site after a burlesque show, where you saw less than you thought you saw. The anticipation was in the idea that I would show something, but I never did. The subscribers never saw more than I wanted them to see. I was professional about my shit. I taped, re-taped, and edited any videos that I posted. And if I planned a live feed... I practiced my butt off, to make sure that everything was... just so. I was open to showing side boob, my ass... but never full-on vagina. I mean, some of those string bikinis and thongs left little to the imagination, but anybody watching me *did* have to use their imagination. Nobody can say they ever saw my coochie or even my nipples."

"Your site was successful?"

She nodded. "Yeah, for somebody who really wasn't showing anything, when there are tons of chicks on there, showing everything their momma gave them. My site was successful. I presented as this upscale girl-next-door type. I would start the videos or live feeds wearing plaid skirts and cardigan sweaters or like an oversized letterman's jacket and really tight cigarette pants."

"Cigarette pants? Never heard of it. What is that?" I was intrigued by her story.

"They're like, okay, imagine a pair of slacks, but with a really, really skinny silhouette. I'm saying, they're tight, and they're cut to ankle length. They have a classic look about them, but then they're tight as hell. Women used to wear them in the fifties and sixties when it was highly inappropriate for women to be overtly sexual. So, they're understated sexy.

"Some days, I would wear a cropped white button-up with a bright red tie and a black pencil skirt. I would slowly undress to reveal whatever I was *modeling* that day. A certain niche of men ate my act up."

"Shit," I allowed. "Cropped white button-up with a black pencil skirt sounds like 'sexy librarian' to me. I can see why some men ate that up. It's like a fantasy. I don't know nothing about the schoolgirl setup... unless you're a pedophile or something. But the sexy librarian? Yeah, she can definitely get it."

"Sexy librarian was the entire vibe," she admitted with a hearty laugh. "I even wore these lens-less tortoise-shell glasses and looked over the top of them, like... all the time. When I first started the account, it was more 'little sister playing dress-up.' I was trying to be sexy, and I think I was failing to everybody, except the super horny, super incel – involuntarily celibate type men. As I got more comfortable and kind of determined what I felt comfortable doing and who I felt comfortable being on the site, my style evolved, and my subscribers picked up."

"You met Elijah Emerson while you were doing your Kitty Yum-Yum thing?"

"Yes. I had a sponsorship where I was asked to attend parties. He was at one of the parties. He came over to my table and talked to me all night. I was totally flattered because the group he came with was in another section of the VIP, acting complete fools. I mean, there was just... debauchery. And he'd decided to forgo that to sit at my table and talk to me."

"Did he know why you were there? Did he know what you did?"

"Not initially. I told him, though. While we sat at the table chatting,

I told him why I was there and who I was. He pulled up my site right there at the table and subscribed."

"What made you... retire Kitty Yum-Yum? Having Key?"

That was when she told me about the way her relationship ended and the intense way that Elijah had tried to both crush her and ruin her livelihood.

# Eight

## Kitari

Two weeks after Labor Day, my life had taken a turn. Elijah had amped up his crusade to serve me with court papers, demanding a DNA test on Key. Unfortunately for him, I wasn't going to be the same fool twice. He'd shown me his hand the first time around when he'd broken up with me and kicked off his campaign of terror. He'd had me served several times with legal documents—documents that required me to leave our home... documents that required me to keep my mouth closed and not talk about the way he had treated me.

Every time I was served by Elijah, it was by some badly dressed, unassuming white person with a look of *intention* in their eyes. They would make eye contact with me, then hurry over and slap the paperwork into my hands.

Either that, or they would sincerely question, "Kitari Miller?"

And I would naively respond, "yes?" then bam! Papers slapped into my hand. But now that I knew better, I could do better.

"How are you holding up?" Kirbie asked while we waited for the waitress to come around to the table and take our orders.

The two of us were having lunch at *Verdadero*, our favorite Mexican restaurant.

"Not well." I let the menu drop from my hands and float down to the tabletop. "I don't even know why I agreed to have lunch today. My appetite is not... appetite-ing."

She commiserated with me, giving me the pouty face. "I know it's not. Has Elijah's wack ass been contacting you?"

"He has. I just keep blocking him. Every number he calls from, I block. I have absolutely no intention of talking to him. I have nothing to say to him. Not after the way he's been acting and the fact that he's constantly talking crap about me on his socials. Saying he never introduced me to his family when he knows that's a damn lie. I've met his mother... more times than I care to remember. I just wish he would fall off the face of the earth."

"Do you think he keeps trying to contact you because he really wants to have a relationship with Key?" She was trying to ask the question gently, but when you didn't want to be bothered with a specific question, there was no good way for the person to ask it.

"I don't give a fuck what he wants!" I spat, barely managing not to stomp my foot like a toddler. "He didn't give a fuck about what I wanted when he sent me to Iredia, then married Mariah. Or when he came back from his honeymoon and made it his life's mission to ruin me. Why is he so worried about a kid now? Knowing that he killed my *Only For Fans* success, does he even ever consider how I feed the baby he's so juiced up to get his hands on?"

"Well, he claims that he didn't know about her."

"What did he need to know about her for?"

"He thinks she's his daughter."

I looked my sister directly in the face. Hazel eyes held the gaze of hazel eyes. "I don't care what he thinks. Key. Is. Not. His." I took a breath. "Kirbie, I know that everybody in our family thinks that I'm just saying that Elijah isn't Key's father because I'm bitter or hurt or something. I'm not. I say it because it's true. She's not his."

"So, why are you fighting so hard against giving this asshole a paternity test? You could do the test, prove she's not his, and get him the hell out of your life for good."

"Because I shouldn't have to prove anything to anybody. If I say she's not his, then that's what it should be." I knew I sounded irrational, but I really didn't care.

"So, you were cheating on Elijah then?"

I wanted to be really pissed with my sister for not dropping it, but I got Kirbie. She was the consummate middle child. She was a fixer. It was killing her that she couldn't fix my situation. I wouldn't even give her enough information to understand my situation. But I didn't even fully understand it myself. I did, but...

"I don't want to talk about it."

It turned out that I didn't have to, because the waitress chose that exact moment to show up to take our orders.

"Has Elijah served you with the papers?" She picked the conversation right back up once the waitress walked away.

"He's trying, but I'm on it." I tapped the stem of the blacked-out sunglasses that sat on top of my head. "I wear these every day. I don't care if it's gloomy outside. I don't make eye contact with anybody. I don't respond to anybody calling out my name in public. He's probably in the process of trying to get my address. Good luck to him, since my condo was purchased under the umbrella of Aunt True's corporation."

"He could always hire somebody to follow you from *Engineered Excellence*."

I sighed. Logically, I knew that Elijah could find me if he put his mind to it. I just didn't want to have to think about that. "That's not a reality that I'm willing to face."

Her eyes went all soft. "But you probably should, Kit Kat. Elijah Emerson controlled you for a long time. He only gave up control so he could marry Mariah Freeman. I feel like if he wants a DNA test on Key, he's not gonna stop until you give him one. And you not wanting to give him one probably puts a battery in his back and makes him want it even more."

She wasn't lying. There was nothing Elijah enjoyed more than watching me succumb to his will.

She watched me silently, clearly picking up on my mood. When she spoke again, it had nothing to do with Elijah Emerson or Key's parentage. "What's up with you and Omari Mann? Are y'all a... *thing* or what?" She wiggled her eyebrows comically.

"We are not a thing," I was quick to inform her, then paused. "Well, we have sex now... but I'm not sure that makes us a thing."

"Y'all are having sex?" Her hazel eyes were wide with wonder. "Uh, I'mma need all the details, Kit Kat."

I chuckled at her thirst for the tea. "Look at your thirsty ass," I teased.

"Uhm, that's your fault. Because just a little while ago, you were all, *Omari and Kitari with the rhyming names? I would never!*"

"You're so dramatic." Her reenactment of our earlier conversation made me laugh loudly.

"You were so dramatic, acting like you couldn't see past the rhyming names... now all you can see is the dick," she jested.

"Okay, so I should clarify. When I said that Omari and I have sex now, that was a bit of an exaggeration. We've had sex once, and it was oral sex. I'm not ready to have... actual sex with anybody. The last time I had actual sex..." I let my thoughts taper off into silence.

"You got pregnant with Key?"

Shrugging my shoulders, I blew past her question. "Anyway, we both needed to release some... tension. So, we took care of each other."

"And that's all it was? Releasing some tension?" Her eyes searched mine.

"What else would it be?" I fronted like Omari wasn't working his way into my system.

"I don't know. Why're you being defensive?"

"I'm not." I fronted some more.

"It's okay if you like him, Kit Kat. It's okay if you let him get close. Every dude is not Elijah."

*No*, I thought to myself. Everyone is *not* Elijah. Some people are much more dangerous to my mental health and well-being.

———

I was served.

Well, *I* wasn't specifically served. I was too savvy to allow those process servers to catch up with me. They did, however, catch up with my mother, at her home. I knew it was my mother who was naive enough to accept the paperwork, because my father was a reformed gambler. He recognized a hustle when he saw one. He never would've admitted to even knowing me, let alone accepted the paperwork. My mother... didn't recognize hustles... at all... ever. Part of that was the reason she'd remained married to my father.

Anyway, the clock was ticking, because Elijah was demanding a paternity test, and he wasn't trying to wait for it.

*I hate him and every single thing about his ass*, I thought to myself as I sat next to Omari at the dining room table of Christian and Genesis Upton.

I wasn't even sure how things had gotten to this point, the point where Gensie and Christian were involved. All I'd done was tell my sister that I needed a lawyer to fight Elijah's request. Now, I sat at an expensive live-wood dining table, with five pairs of eyes trained on me.

"So, Chance and I had his attorney look into the court order," Kirbie began. "And he didn't seem too confident about getting an injunction against the paternity test."

"Damn," I muttered.

"But people with money can make the law bend to their will," Genesis commented. "So, I asked Chris Cross to see what he could do. Like, could we pay somebody to make this... disappear."

"Can we?" I questioned, a ray of hope now sparked.

Genesis looked over at her husband, and he took the floor.

"My attorney doesn't feel like we can get an injunction that can prevent the DNA testing all together, but he does feel like we can put the burden of proof on dude," Christian relayed. "Like, he can't just go around requesting that women give him paternity tests without just cause. So, we can ask him to prove just cause. Like, does Key's birthday match up with a timeframe that makes it plausible that he could've fathered her? Can he prove that you all were *together* to even produce Key—stuff like that."

I was silent as I thought about the information that Christian had just provided.

"No shade, Kitari. I just have to say this, lil mama. This is some of the wildest shit I've ever heard of in my life," Chance commented. "Normally, it's chicks on social media claiming that such-n-such is their kid's father, demanding a paternity test, while the dude in question denies. Denies. Denies. If you know Key isn't his, I don't get why you don't just give him the fucking paternity test and get him out of your life."

"I have my reasons," I mumbled.

"Is it because you're not one-hundred percent sure that he isn't the father?" Chance pushed.

And even though Chance was the one to pose the question, I could see everybody at the table waiting with bated breath for my response. I could also feel annoyance begin creeping through me.

"How many times—" I began before being cut off by Omari.

"Yo," he said, in that deep, raspy DMX voice of his, "we appreciate everything—all the research, all time, energy, and effort that you've put into helping Kitari find a solution. But the two of us will take it from here. It seems to me that every time this dude's name comes up or that Key's paternity has come up, Kitari has reiterated over and over again that Elijah Emerson is not the damn father. Yet, here we are, and y'all are asking her... again." He paused. "I do like the idea of making this dude prove that he *could* be the father before Key has to be subjected to getting swabbed. So, I'll present that to *my* attorney, and we'll see where it gets us. Let's go, Kitari."

"Uhm, excuse me, sir," Kirbie began. "Kitari is my sister. I feel like you're making it seem like I don't have her best interest at heart."

"That's not my intention, little mama. My intention is to protect Kitari. That's it. That's all. I'm about making sure she's good. And I'm watching her sit here feeling exposed, yet still unheard. It's clear that all of y'all think this cat is the father or could be the father, regardless of the fact that she's told y'all otherwise. She needs a different kind of energy. I'mma do that for her. Let's go, Kitari."

*He wants to protect you.* Inner Kitari repeated Omari's words. It had been so long since somebody offered to protect me, since I'd felt protected. I pushed back from the table.

———

Her hand moved through my hair, haphazardly parting sections with her nails so that her fingertips briefly came in contact with my scalp. Her touch was giving me the human contact, care, and concern that had only recently been reintroduced into my life by Omari.

Not to act like Key didn't do her part with the sweet kisses and hugs that affected me in ways only love from your child could. Love and adoration from Key gave me goosebumps and warm fuzzies. My daughter had the 'human contact' part on lock. But I couldn't lean on Key. I couldn't expect Key to offer care and concern. I'd accepted long ago that I would just have to learn how to live without that. But then God decided that I wasn't going out like that, because he'd sent Omari Mann. And Omari came in like a lake effect breeze, skirting the surface of the waters of Lake Michigan, cool and refreshing. Unexpected, yet unignorable.

"Are you letting him protect you, Kit Kat? If that's what he has clearly stated that he wants to do, are you allowing him to do that?"

My aunt and I were in the sitting room of her house, lounging on the cushy sofa. I'd often found myself at aunt True's home over the years, whenever I needed a non-judgmental sounding board.

My mother could only relate to people who thought like her and moved like her. Sometimes, a girl needed to talk to somebody who could see the big picture, as well as keep an open mind. My aunt was in the business of building relationships with professional athletes. There wasn't a lot that shocked her or knocked her off her square.

"The last time somebody acted like the moves they were making were all to protect me..." I didn't even bother finishing the statement.

I had never told anybody about the things I'd gone through when I left the island of Iredia and returned to the home that Elijah and I shared in Londynville, Kentucky... except True. She was the only one who knew the details, the only one who knew the secrets I kept buried deep inside.

"That was a different situation, and you were dealing with a... couple of psychopaths and sociopaths. Omari Mann doesn't seem diabolical."

"Doesn't matter," I murmured.

"Doesn't it?" she countered. "Doesn't it matter if a healthy, conscientious man wants to protect you?"

I circumvented the question. "He put his lawyer on speaker while he told him about my situation. I mean... as much as he *could* tell him, because it's not like Omari has many... any details. Anyway, the attorney was very thorough. He explained that he agreed with Christian Upton's attorney. We could put Elijah in a position where he would have to prove that there's reasonable evidence to suggest that Key is his before he could get his paternity test." I forced out a weighty sigh. "But it would require me to provide Key's birth certificate and details and... it's just not worth it. If I'm gonna do all that, jump through all the hoops, it would be way less dramatic to just let Elijah have his DNA test."

"I know when Key was born, there were threats and accusations thrown around, but what I told you then still stands, niecy pooh. I. Will. Protect. You. I will build a fortress around you and Key if I have to. I will keep you safe. It has always felt a little like you don't trust me."

"It wasn't you, Auntie. I didn't trust anybody... even myself. My mind was telling me crazy shi... stuff to do. People were constantly lying to me." I fought back tears.

I hated remembering that period. The memories were filled with pain, and even more so with fear and shame... fear of not knowing what would happen next, shame of what I had become, shame over the fact that I couldn't cope. I was ashamed about what I had done instead of coping. The choices I had made that affected not only me, but Key.

"I want you to stop beating yourself up for your trauma responses. The person making the decisions that you made back then wasn't whole and healthy Kitari. It was traumatized, confused, and devastated Kitari. She did the best she could do--"

"Well, the best *she* could do left a lot to be desired." I interrupted with a mutter.

"Not true. She managed to get herself and her newborn daughter out of that situation. She managed to reach out for help."

"For a rescue." Another utterance escaped my lips.

"So what? Everybody needs rescuing every now and again. And anyway, you and Key are my nieces. I don't give a damn if I have to rescue y'all one hundred times a freaking week. I'm doing it because y'all are family. And family is there for family."

"If I never said it before, Auntie True, thank you. Thank you for coming through for me and Key. Thank you for moving mountains to get me out of that situation."

"You have said it before, and you don't ever have to say it again. But you are welcome. And it was my pleasure. I had been waiting for your call for months. I was... relieved when it finally came."

"I was relieved. I wish I never put myself in that situation. Four years later, I'm still in a situation."

"You can get out of that situation any day of the week. I will throw every resource in my arsenal at this problem."

"It isn't just about me," I defended. "This affects Key, too."

"The secret you keep so tight to your chest isn't even your secret to keep, if you wanna be really honest about it, niecy pooh. You don't have anything to hide. They do. They're the sick ones." She sucked her teeth. "The sociopaths in sheep's clothing."

I sighed, which did not deter her.

"You know what they say about secrets—that a secret can be a promise... but it can be a prison, too."

"Say less," I basically whispered, as the truth of her words settled into the very fiber of me.

The secret of Key's parentage was keeping me in bondage. I had to wonder if Key was benefitting from me keeping it or if irrational fear was just punking me into inaction.

# NINE

OMARI

The last home pre-season game was in the books. Chicago Bison 93, Santa Fe Coyotes 88. It was a good game for me. I played twelve minutes in the first half and sixteen minutes in the second. I played like I had my sea legs under me. The workouts with Gideon Show had definitely paid off. Surprise consumed me about how tired I *wasn't* after about ten treks up and down the court.

"Good game, Big Vet," one of the young players, whose name I couldn't remember, called out to me as I exited the locker room as he entered.

It didn't get past me that some of the players had media obligations I didn't have. Even though I'd played thirty minutes of the forty-eight and had managed to score eight points and have three assists, there were no reporters waiting to talk to me when I walked off the court. Nobody had questions for me... or even interest in me.

I sighed. I knew it shouldn't bother me, and mostly, it didn't... but a little... it did. I bent the corner, barely registering the people crowded into the hallway. I was focused on getting to my truck. My eyes scanned the area, mostly so that I didn't bump into anybody or anything, but then they caught the gaze of hazel eyes—the intense gaze of hazel eyes from a body leaned against the wall, staring directly at me.

*What is she doing here?*

I made a beeline toward her. "You got press credentials or something that I don't know about? What are you doing here?"

"I have something better than press credentials," Kitari confided with a smirk. "I've got connections. I'm close with the wife of the most famous person in the city."

Knowing she was referring to Genesis Upton and her husband, Christian, I didn't bother with comments or questions about it. "And you used this connection to come and meet me here?" I gestured around the hallway under the stadium where locker rooms and press rooms were housed.

"You played a really good game tonight." A wide grin split her pretty face. "Really good. You did not look thirty-five years old out there."

I returned the smile. "Thanks. I can honestly say that I didn't feel it either."

Her eyes swept down my body, taking in the bag I held. Then, they moved over the crowded corridor, before landing on mine. "You about to head home?"

"Yeah, unless you have other plans."

"Nah." Her response came without hesitation. "Just wondering if I can tag along."

Could she tag along? Did a bear shit in the woods? Hell yeah, she could tag along, anytime she wanted.

"Didn't I already tell you to ask for whatever you want, and I'll give it to you? That includes me."

She repeated my words in a whisper. "That includes you."

"Where's my little mama tonight?" I asked as my truck ate up the few miles between the stadium and my house.

"With my parents. I wanted to... spend some uninterrupted time with you, so I asked if they would keep her."

I nodded while keeping my eyes on the road.

"I want to talk to you, and I don't want little ears to hear what I have to say."

"Say less," I responded, and we drove the remainder of the distance to my place in silence.

When we got to my place, Kitari settled herself on the balcony of my bedroom. It was early October. The days were still nice, featuring warm, pleasant weather, but the nights could be chilly. She didn't seem to notice, making herself comfortable as she stared out at the lake. I left her there while I showered, again, then threw on joggers, a hoodie, and slides. I took the seat opposite her.

"You hungry, sweetheart?" I questioned.

She pulled the hazel eyes that I admired so much from the lake and placed them on me. "Maybe in a minute."

There was a heaviness surrounding her. That wasn't unusual for Kitari. For as much as she brought light into my life, she was often weighed down with something that... belied that.

"Elijah Emerson had me served with papers demanding a DNA test again today," she stated, her voice completely devoid of emotion. "He and his lawyer feel like I'm stalling."

"Are you?" That seemed to be the only reasonable response to her proclamation.

"I am," she confessed. "But not for the reason he thinks." She heaved out a tortured sigh. "Elijah Emerson isn't Key's father."

"You've told me that several times, baby girl. I know that. I believe you."

If I were being honest with myself, I would have to admit that the tears were a surprise. Kitari was the stoic type. I'd seen her get teary eyed, but I'd never seen her full-on cry. Low key, I never wanted to see her cry.

"What's making you cry, sweetheart? The reality of the situation or the what ifs?"

"Both, but mostly the reality. I can't give Elijah the DNA test without talking to him first." She gave a humorless chuckle. "He doesn't deserve it, because he's the one who made the whole situation a public spectacle. I'm not on social media, but I know he's been posting stuff about me... and about Key. And even though he has *never*—since the moment I met him—ever given me a heads up about what was coming down the pike, I don't wanna be like him. I want to be the opposite of him. I wanna be on my Michelle Obama and go high..." she paused, "even though his bitch ass doesn't deserve it."

"Ay, what does your *going high* look like?"

"I contacted him today. Told him that I think we should get together and talk. I told him that after we speak, he can have his DNA test."

"Did he agree?"

"Yeah." She sighed. "They have a bye-week at the end of the month. He's gonna come to Chicago."

"How do you feel about all of this?"

"Like I've been keeping somebody else's secret and carrying around somebody else's shame. I'm ready to give it back."

"Key is four years old, right?" I asked.

Kitari nodded.

"Then, it's time."

She nodded again, her eyes never leaving the water. "You know that thing you do, where you hold me in your arms all tight and stuff?" She didn't wait for a response from me. "I'mma need you to do that tonight."

I opened my arms and waited while she stood from the chair, walked over to me, and arranged herself in my lap, straddling me. Her arms snaked around my neck, while she buried her face in my shoulder. She didn't need to use her words; what she needed from me was evident. I made sure that my embrace was firm but not overly tight as I stroked her back.

"You're gonna be cool, mama. I'mma make sure of it. I got you."

Kitari heaved sobs. I had no idea what was so heavy in her life. All I knew was that it had something to do with Key and her conception. And I knew that I was going to protect Kitari and Key from whatever bullshit Elijah Emerson would try to bring their way.

I held Kitari for an indeterminate amount of time. After a while, her sobs decreased until they turned into whimpers, and not too long after that, her breathing evened out, and we sat on my balcony in silence.

"I'm not crying over Elijah," she announced into the stillness of the night.

"I know," I assured her.

I knew that whatever it was about the situation that troubled her had less to do with Elijah and more to do with Key.

"I cried all the tears I ever planned to cry over him back in Londynville, Kentucky. It's just that looking back on that entire period in my life makes me... furious. It pisses me off. The way I was treated by..." She let her thought trail off, but her lips were still poked out in a sensual pout.

Leaning in ever so slightly, I kissed them, mashing mine to hers. It was a gentle act. At the same time, there was nothing gentle about it. Her brown orbs crashed into mine when our lips parted.

"How do you always seem to know what I need?"

"I don't know. You think we've got some kind of crazy connection?"

"I *know* we've got some kind of crazy connection... and I'm not mad at it." Shifting on my lap, she spoke again. "I want to be closer to you." She pushed out a small sigh. "I need to be closer to you."

She didn't need to say anything else. I knew what she meant. I stood with her still in my lap, her arms once again snaking around my neck.

When we were at the foot of my bed, I set her down on her feet. Without hesitation, Kitari began to strip. Once she was naked, she climbed under the blankets. It only took me a minute or so to remove my own clothing, grab a condom from my nightstand drawer, and slide in beside her.

"It's been a minute for you, right?" I pulled her into my arms.

"Yeah." Her hazel eyes were as big as saucers as she stared at me. "Since before Key."

The expression on her face told me that she didn't want me to harp on the fact that she hadn't had sex in over four years. So, I didn't. I played it through. I positioned her on her back, then moved between her legs, spreading them as I made myself comfortable. The atmosphere was thick. I decided to thin it out. "Yo, you're giving me your 'post-Key' virginity?"

She chuckled lightly, which had been my intent. "Yeah. Something like that." She placed her manicured hand on my chest. "So, treat me like a virgin, Omari." Her eyes blinked rapidly. "Be gentle with me. Don't be bending me all up and acting like I'm some kind of Olympic gymnast."

It was my turn to chuckle. "I got you, K. That'll come later," I teased, then stared down at her. "With your pretty ass. You're so fucking pretty, girl." My head shook back and forth.

"Omari..." she started, a blush creeping slowly up on her cheeks.

I didn't let her sit in that moment. Instead, I lowered my head and captured her lush mouth. Kissing her lips, I used my tongue to encourage her to open her mouth. I lavished her mouth for a few moments, before trailing my kisses down her jawline to her neck. Kitari was sensitive as hell on her neck, and I used that fact to my advantage, sucking and nipping her there.

She was so beautiful to me. Every inch of her commanded my exploration. I pulled her earlobe between my teeth and sucked that, while my hands traveled the length of her body, stopping to massage her breasts, before moving across her ample thighs.

Once my exploration made it to her sweetest spot, her arousal was evident from the cream that coated my fingertips. I removed my hand and rubbed the head of my dick against her clit, until she moaned for me. Slowly, I inserted myself inch by inch into what I could only describe as Kitari's own personal torture chamber. Her walls suctioned my dick like it had personally offended her, wrenching and wrestling him in its grip.

"You okay?" The words came out on a groan, because the fit was so fucking tight, I could barely stand it. I could only imagine what she was feeling and thinking.

Whatever her response was to me, it was indiscernible, mangled and garbled with a moan. I took that to mean that she was cool. Pressing forward slowly, I pushed into her. The walls of her vagina expanded, offering me a bit more space to move.

Again and again, I rocked into her while intermittently dropping kisses on every part of her that came into contact with my mouth. Her pussy gripped me like pliers, squeezing the shit out of me in the best possible way, like she always wanted me inside of her. She moaned and held me tightly as she experienced sensations I knew she hadn't felt in literal years.

"You feel good as shit." I pulled out only long enough to flip her over. Wrapping my arm around her waist, I tugged until she was on all fours. Then I reinserted myself back into the warmness of her middle.

Kitari threw her ass back at me, softly chanting, "Yes. Yes," as each of my thrusts landed.

Placing my hand on her lower back, I pressed down until she followed my lead, giving me the perfect arch. I stroked her out until I could feel my nut starting to bubble up. So, I picked up speed, long stroking her until she cried out, while her breath simultaneously caught in her throat. My load shot into the condom, as her pussy contracted around me, signaling her own orgasm.

I felt Kitari roll over while I was in the space between being asleep and awake. "Omari."

My eyes came open slowly, and I was faced with pitch blackness. Unlike Kitari's bedroom, my bedroom featured black-out curtains.

Although I couldn't see her, I could feel her. I reached out and pulled her into my body. My head rested atop hers. "Aren't you supposed to be asleep?"

"I was." She stretched. "Seeing Elijah. Facing... my past is... a lot."

"The idea of seeing him is messing with your sleep?"

"Yeah," she admitted with a sigh.

I laid a kiss in her hair.

"If you're home and available when this meeting with Elijah happens, would you be willing to... be there?"

My expression arranged itself into a frown, even though she couldn't see it with the room being so dark. "You think I would let you go through something that has you worked up and losing sleep by yourself, if it can be helped? Let me know the date, and I'll definitely see what I can do."

"Okay." She snuggled into my chest. "Thank you."

"Not a problem," I assured her.

An hour later, Kitari was sound asleep, while I lay in bed, my thoughts refusing to leave me alone.

———

"That's one bitch ass nigga," Gideon commented, looking over at me from across the table. He set his phone face down.

The two of us had decided to grab a bite to eat after our workout. While we waited for our food to arrive, he'd watched a video Elijah Emerson posted about his situation with Kitari a few days earlier.

I nodded at his assessment of dude because it was a waste of time to dispute the truth.

"The way he's coming for your girl, you must wanna fuck this nigga up something awful."

"Dog." I chuckled humorlessly, with a shake of my head. "Can't do it. So, for now, I'm fucking him up monetarily. Had my attorney file a cease-and-desist order. Let's see if he violates it. If he does, my girl'll have his money in her purse."

"What kinda low-life motherfucker runs around bad mouthing the mother of his child on social media like this? Is it any wonder she keeps the kid away from him? His ass is toxic with a fucking capital T."

"She doesn't keep the kid away from him," I corrected. "The kid's not his."

Gideon looked over at me with his face comically screwed. "Bro. What?" he questioned.

"My girl's daughter isn't his."

"Well, why does he think it's his kid?"

I stared at him. It didn't take a scientist to figure out why a man would think he had fathered a child.

"Okay, they were fucking. Does he not believe that she would've tricked off on him? What does he think? That he got the magic stick?" He laughed. "Delusional niggas. Clearly, he can't accept that nowadays women cheat the fuck back. Shit, he oughtta be giving her kudos for not trying to pin the baby on him. Instead, he's on *InstaChat*, dragging her through the mud for not pinning the baby on him? I'll never under-stand some of these dudes."

"Word." I agreed, perusing the menu. "And even if he does think the baby is his, where's the benefit to airing all the shit out on social media? This dude acts like shorty won't ever be old enough to read and see the things he's said about her mother."

"Bitch-osity at its finest." Gideon's head wagged back and forth while his face wore a scowl.

"Say less. I'm counting down to the day that she gives his ass the DNA test so we can be done with it," I muttered, looking around for our waitress. I was hungry and ready to order.

"We?" he probed, his eyebrows so high they were practically touching his hairline. "We? You speakin' French now, Big Vet?"

The players on the team had taken to calling me "Big Vet" because I was old as hell and had been in the league for longer than most of them had been out of grade school.

I couldn't help the smirk that came across my face.

"I thought old girl was just a *friend*."

"Ay, don't judge me 'cause I'm ride or die for my peoples. You must suck as a friend."

He laughed aloud. "You're lyin', Big Vet. I knew she was more than your friend when I saw the video that lame motherfucker posted of y'all in the grocery store. The one where she was like, 'come on, babes. Your mom is waiting on us.'" He sweetened his voice and raised it twelve octaves in a bad impersonation of Kitari.

I pretended to be engrossed with the menu, even though I knew exactly what I was ordering.

Gideon laughed again. "It's cool, my G. I'mma let you live. She's a good look for you. And that whole incident in the grocery store proved that she keeps a calm head. That's what we need in this lifestyle." He paused. "Well, maybe not you as much as the rest of us. You're *mature* and shit." He said the word mature like it left a bad taste in his mouth.

It was my turn to laugh aloud.

"The rest of us are out here just doing shit. On our socials, at these clubs... just wildin'. We need a counterpart that keeps a cool head under pressure."

"You getting deep, G."

He looked around the restaurant slowly, then shrugged his shoulders. "I don't know, man. I look around, and I see images of what I'm supposed to want—a woman with an ass too fat to fit in my hands, and a waist smaller than my fucking wrist. I don't know. Somehow... that shit don't seem... right." He sighed. "I mean, the optics will have you blowing the fuck up on your socials. But in real life, I'mma be wondering if my girl's internal organs are crushed up or some shit."

I had to snigger because I understood exactly what he was saying.

"I'm saying. Does that shit look healthy? When we get old, am I gonna have to wipe her ass because she fucked something up in her twenties, trying to look like a Kardashian? I don't know, man. I don't want no wife that's a flex right now but a damn invalid twenty years from now."

"I hear you, dawg," I assured him. "I hear you."

Gideon sucked his teeth. "Your shorty might have some shit with her, as far as Elijah Emerson is concerned, but once y'all get the paternity test, the drama will be in the rearview mirror. Light work. Some of these women... and men, shit, let's be honest—they *really* got some shit with them. You should make sure to lock her pretty ass down." He paused. "Ay, she got a sister or something?"

This dude jumped from one subject to the next like it wasn't a thing. "Actually, she does. You know Parker is engaged to her sister."

"Damn." His eyes got wide. "Yeah, she does have those same light eyes as his girl. Yeah, I can see the resemblance. They look alike. I shoulda put that together." He took a beat. "They ain't got no other sisters?"

"They do have a younger sister, but I doubt she's ready for you, G. She's young, 'bout twenty-two or so."

"Slide her my number," he requested. "Does she look like the other two? Light eyes? Dark skin? She mature for her age?"

"I ain't fuckin' with you, G." I laughed out loud.

"What? I'm serious. Gimme the plug."

———

The night before Key was scheduled to be swabbed for the DNA test, Kitari called me via video chat, after I made it home from the game. I was chilling on the balcony, in her favorite spot, looking out at the water and nursing a bottle of beer. Although it wasn't cold, I had the fire pit going to make it more comfortable.

"Hey, gorgeous," I stated, looking into her face.

"Hey, handsome." She gave me a small, forced smile.

"Key down for bed?"

"She is."

"What did you tell her was happening tomorrow?" I questioned.

"I told her that she's going to the doctor to get her mouth checked out. I told her that it won't hurt. And that once she's done, her aunt Kinzie is going to take her to school."

"So, you're bringing Kinzie with you?"

"I'm bringing Kinzie and Aunt True. Kinzie'll be there to entertain and keep an eye on Key while I talk to Elijah. Then once the test is done, Kinzie's gonna drop Key off at school for me. It should be like... a regular day for Key. I mean, I'm hoping that she won't pick up on any... weirdness from me, but I don't see how she won't. I'm already a mess. I can only imagine how crazy I'm gonna be tomorrow." She huffed out a sigh. "Even though I'm bugging and having multiple panic attacks, I'm glad to finally be confronting this. I've been holding on to this--"

I watched tears flow down her cheeks.

"Yo, I hope you're up for company, because I'm on my way."

She sniffled hard and swiped at the tears. "No, Omari. Please don't come here. I didn't call you to cry in your face. I called you to talk."

"Why you called is irrelevant. If you need me, I'm heading your way. And you seem to need me."

"No," she repeated, this time more forcefully. "I need to talk to you, and I won't be able to do it in person."

"Why not?" I wanted to know.

"Because," she whispered, "I never talk about this out loud... ever. I don't even like thinking about it."

I stayed silent.

"Tomorrow, I'm going to have to tell Elijah and his lawyer how I know for sure that Key isn't his," she choked out, still whispering. "I want you to hear the story first. I can't let you hear it when he hears it. You need to know what you're walking into."

"Okay." I agreed over the lump that was sitting in my throat. My imagination was running wild with thoughts of the story she was about to tell me about Key's conception.

"Okay," she repeated, taking a deep breath.

I jumped in before she could speak again, because there was one thing I needed to know. "Baby, is Key the product of rape?"

Though her head was shaking in the negative, the trail of tears that made their way down her face made her answer hard to believe.

"It's complicated." She croaked.

I could feel myself getting choked up at the pain radiating from my girl. "Please, baby. Please, let me come to you."

Her head continued to shake in the negative. "I'll never get the story out. And I have to get the story out, Omari. I can't let Elijah see me fall apart." She seemed to toughen up right before my eyes. "I won't let Elijah see me fall apart."

"Fuck that nigga!" My tone was evidence of my frustration.

She nodded, then cleared her throat. "Right. Fuck him." She took a deep breath. "Okay, so when I found out that Elijah had married Mariah Freeman after sending me out of the country, I was devastated. I caught the first possible flight back to Londynville, Kentucky, where we lived at the time. Aunt True had told me to leave my stuff in Londynville and just let her fly me to Chicago... but I wouldn't listen. I wanted my belongings.

"When I got to the community we stayed in, the guards at the gate told me that I wasn't allowed on the property. Everything I owned, with the exception of what I had in my luggage, was in that house. I couldn't believe that Elijah was trying to deny me access. It was like, all of the hurt, anger, exhaustion, deception... like everything came to a head right in that moment. I drove my truck right through the gates."

I didn't react to her admission. "I probably would've done the same thing," I told her.

"I got to the house and used my keys to get in. I was out for blood. I couldn't believe Elijah did that to me. Of course, the house was empty, because Elijah was on his honeymoon. I calmed down enough to where I could think straight and started packing. I was sitting in the middle of the floor in the master bedroom when the police arrived."

"The guards at the gatehouse called the cops on you?" I probed.

"They did." She wasn't making eye contact with me. She was looking down, like she was embarrassed.

As far as I was concerned, she didn't have anything to be embarrassed about.

"The police were really nice, though. I explained to them that I lived there... had lived there for over two years. I showed them my license, which had that address on it and everything. I explained to them that it was the home of the Londynville Leopards wide receiver, Elijah Emerson, and that he had sent me out of the country while he married somebody else, then refused to allow me on the property. I think the cops were embarrassed for me. They did still try to put me out, but I called Aunt True, and she got her lawyer on the phone. Legally, they couldn't put me out. So, eventually, they left."

"Did you stay there, or did you pack and head to Chicago?" I asked the question, already knowing the answer.

"I didn't leave. I went into the closet with the intention of packing my stuff, but instead, I ended up having a breakdown." She sighed. "I stayed in the house for over a week. Each day, I destroyed a different room"

"Good girl," I mumbled. "I hope you fucked his shit up."

"I fucked his shit up, my shit up. The dog's shit got fucked up. Everything in there got destroyed. Each day, Elijah had me served with a different court order.

On about the ninth or tenth day, Elijah showed up. A blind rage came over me. In retrospect, I thank God for the fact that I couldn't remember the combination to the gun safe. I tried every set of numbers I could think of. I could not get that safe open. But I did have access to my taser. So, when that low-down ass bastard came into the kitchen, I tased him."

I chuckled lightly.

"He brought his brother, Elvis, with him. My short-term plan was to kill Elijah. I mean, he was on the floor after I tased him, and we were in the kitchen. All I needed was a knife. I planned to stab him to death, but Elvis walked in and distracted me. I tried to tase him, too, but I didn't have the element of surprise, and he knocked the taser out of my hand. Then, he overpowered me and barricaded me in one of the closets."

"What do you mean, he overpowered you? This motherfucker put his hands on you?"

"I mean, he did. But I think it was more so to keep me from hurting his brother more than I already had. He was... rough with me, but he didn't hurt me."

"Still..."

"Please let me get the story out, Omari."

"Okay. Go 'head."

"After about a half an hour or so, Elvis comes to the closet. He tells me that Elijah is prepared to file charges against me for the destruction of his property and for assault. He tells me that it's in my best interest to leave the premises. I started thinking about all of the court orders. Plus, I just keep thinking that possession is nine-tenths of the law. I know that if I leave the house, Elijah will make sure that I never come back inside again, and I don't have anywhere to go. So--"

"I thought you were headed home to Chicago after you got your stuff?" I interrupted.

She sighed. "I was. But then I started thinking about how Elijah was trying to dispose of me, and I was letting him. I was thinking about how he'd played me, and I didn't want him to just... get off the hook. I had given him *years* of my life. He didn't get to just... dismiss me." She paused. "I'm not saying my thinking was right, Omari. Quite the contrary. I realize that I wasn't thinking straight. I wasn't thinking logically. And me staying there... in Londynville was the reason that everything that happened after that night happened. I only have myself to blame, because if I had gotten my stuff and flown back to Chicago, I wouldn't have been in the predicament I found myself in."

"Okay."

"I told Elvis that I wasn't leaving because I didn't have anywhere to go. He offered to help me. He's the pastor of a large church in Londynville, well-known in that town and in the black community. That's why I trusted him. I felt like he had resources. Well, he helps me get all of my suitcases and hustles me out of the house, while Elijah watches and makes all these threats about making me wish I'd never been born. Elvis gets me into his truck, then he takes me to a women's shelter."

I didn't know whether to be surprised or not. Part of me felt like if Elijah's ass was as shady as he was, none of his family members should've been trusted.

"I freaked out. I'm not from money, Omari. I mean, I lived good with Elijah, but I've already told you that my mom struggled. She struggled, but I've never not had a roof over my head. I wasn't cut out to live in a shelter. So, I wouldn't get out of the truck. He starts trying to drag me out, and I start fighting him. Apparently, he had a relationship with this shelter or something because the workers came out and started trying to help him get away from me. I was going crazy, but in the midst of my breakdown, I basically begged him to put me in a hotel, just for the night, knowing that Aunt True would get me back to Chicago. Nope. He and the workers get me and my stuff out of the truck, and he drives off."

I watched her cry on my screen. "Little mama," I said softly.

"One of the worst days of my life, but things actually went downhill from there. Omari, I've lost some parts of this story. I don't remember a lot about that shelter. I don't know if that's my brain's way of protecting me from the trauma or what. The main thing I remember is trying to get in touch with my Aunt True because, somehow, I lost my phone, or didn't have service or something. I don't know how long I was there or anything, probably a day or so. Anyway, this one woman there kept taunting me about Elijah. And let me tell you, she had the right one, because I tried to rip her apart."

"Wow."

"I don't know what happened, because the bitches on that girl's trip were taunting me as the video of Elijah getting married played, and I kept my head. I don't know what made me lose my temper on that one lady at the shelter."

"Probably the stress."

"I don't know. All I know is that the staff at the shelter called the police on me. Apparently, as I was beating the lady, I kept screaming about how I just wanted everyone to leave me alone and let me die. I guess I kept saying that I wanted to die, or that I hated life or something. All I know... is that when the police came, they did a fifty-one fifty on me. I was taken immediately to the psych ward of the nearest hospital and handcuffed to the bed. I honestly believe that I was in the middle of a psychotic break, because if I had been in my right mind, that would've been the perfect time to reach out to Aunt True for help. But I didn't."

"Why do you think that you didn't reach out to her?" I couldn't help asking.

She shrugged her shoulders. "I'm not sure. I don't know if I was embarrassed or what. Maybe the thought never entered my mind because I thought I could handle things. I think I thought that I could handle things. Nothing seemed real, Omari. Nothing seemed real. It didn't seem real that Elijah could have or would have sent me out of the country with literal strangers and then married somebody else. It didn't seem real that he tried to evict me from our home or that I tore up that same home or that I tased Elijah until he was writhing on the kitchen floor in pain or that I beat some woman to the point that the police had to be called. Or that the police literally drove me to the hospital for a psychiatric evaluation. Nothing seemed real. It was like I was watching a movie of my life. I was watching Kitari Miller go through these things, but that was separate from what I was experiencing."

"Damn."

"I don't know how long I was at the hospital. Again, memory repression or whatever. I don't know what they were giving me, medication wise or what they were doing to me. All I know is one day I woke up, and I wasn't in the hospital anymore. I didn't know where the hell I was, but it looked like a bedroom, and Elijah's brother, Elvis, was there. He was sitting in a chair that was facing the bed, watching me. He started telling me how God had convicted his heart about leaving me at the shelter. He searched and searched for me. When he finally found me at the hospital, he knew that he was supposed to bring me home with him and help get me back on my feet."

"He's Key's father?" I asked. It was clear as day to me, that the predatory ass pastor had taken a confused Kitari to his home and inserted himself into her life and into her body.

Her shoulders started to shake. "He was giving me so many drugs, Omari. Their mother, Mrs. Emerson—Elijah and Elvis' mother is a nurse practitioner. She had access to drugs, and she was giving him things to give me that kept me... spaced out. And while he was plying me with drugs, he was being kind to me. I didn't realize it at the time, but he was grooming me into a relationship with him." She sniffled and swiped at tears, again. "When you asked if Key is the product of rape, I can't say that she is. The sex was consensual, but I wasn't in my right mind, so how could it have been consensual? I liked it, though. I craved it. I thought I loved Elvis, and I thought he loved me. But he was a sick and demented person. Nobody knew I was at his house, except his diabolical ass mother. He was basically holding me hostage. In a sense, I was his sex slave."

"He kept you locked up in his house?"

"He did." She nodded. "I mean, I could go around the house, but I couldn't leave it. He would say it was because he worried too much about me. He would tell me that I was too fragile, and he didn't trust the world with me. When I would push, he would give me 'medicine' that would knock me out for days. When I would wake up, he would tell me that I had an episode, and blacked out. And my blackouts were the reason he didn't want me leaving the house."

"Fuck," I muttered. I wanted to kill *Elvis*, wherever the fuck he was. I wanted to kill that dude.

"When I started suffering from morning sickness, Mrs. Emerson brought me some home pregnancy tests. Once they came back positive, they stopped drugging me, but I could tell that they were both scared."

"I guess so. How were they gonna explain that the good pastor had not only gotten his brother's ex-girlfriend pregnant, but also the ex-girlfriend who was mentally unstable?"

"I would hear them whisper arguing. Mrs. Emerson wanted to take me out for an abortion. Elvis wanted me to have the baby. They spent months concocting plans and changing them."

"If you were with them for months, where did your family think you were? Were they looking for you?"

"I didn't know if they were looking for me or not. My mom had called me shortly before I caught a flight out of Iredia, and we got into a huge fight. She was trying to offer me advice on how to deal with Elijah's betrayal. But how could I listen to her when I didn't even respect the way that she handled my father's betrayal? He betrayed her every time he gambled his paycheck and her paycheck and the bill money away. We ended up getting into a screaming match. She probably convinced herself and the rest of the family that I was avoiding them."

I exhaled heavily.

"Once they stopped plying me with drugs, and I was able to get sober, all I wanted was to get the hell out of there. My phone was long gone. Elvis had alarms and codes on all the windows and doors. It was a fortress."

"Kitari," I said softly.

"I was in a nightmare. I'd gotten myself into a really bad situation, all because I didn't just go back to Chicago when I had a chance."

"Even if your mother was convinced that you were avoiding her, did your sisters really believe that you were avoiding them?"

"I told you that Kirbie and I weren't close at that time. She was in college, probably living her hot girl summer. She probably assumed that I was off somewhere doing Kitari. Kinzie was young. She probably believed my mom's version of things. My aunt True was looking for me, though. She told me later that she called every hospital in Londynville... and the one hospital had a record of me being admitted there but no record of me being released. I don't know how Elvis got me out of that hospital, but there was no record of me being released to him. Probably one of his parishioners worked there or something. True filed a lawsuit against the hospital... and won. That money is in a trust for Key."

"They admitted negligence?"

"They had a record of me being admitted, but no record of me being released. No signed paperwork saying that I'd checked myself out. No video of me leaving the property. They *were* negligent."

"How'd you get away from the looney toon ass dude?"

"I didn't know what to do. I was suffering from severe morning sickness, mixed with extreme depression. I literally wanted to die. I tried to jump out of the second-floor window."

"Word?" I was shocked. "You didn't see any other way out, huh?"

She shook her head. "I didn't. And all I kept thinking was that the baby I was carrying was gonna keep him and his psychotic ass mother in my life forever. The alarms went off, alerting the entire house that I opened the window, and that plan was a fail. When that didn't work, I took an entire bottle of pills. Mrs. Emerson found me. They rushed me to the hospital and had my stomach pumped. After that, they watched me like a hawk and put me back on 'medicine.' Then they made me sign something giving Elvis full custody of the baby at birth. The papers revoked my parental rights, based on the fact that I was emotionally unstable and suicidal."

"Shit, baby. So, dude was drugging you, fucking you, and holding you hostage? Then, he forced you to sign over your rights to the unborn child? Shit!"

"When I was about thirty weeks or so, I started having really excruciating abdominal pain. Of course, they assumed that I was faking and blew me off for over a day. When they finally realized that I needed medical attention, they took me to the hospital. I had an infection that was causing me to have contractions. The doctors thought they could treat the infection and keep Key inside, but they couldn't stop the contractions, and my blood pressure started going through the roof.

"I delivered Key early, and the second that I laid eyes on her, everything dark in my life became light."

"How'd you get away from dude and his momma? How'd you end up with custody of Key?"

"Later on in the day, after I had Key, a social worker or somebody came into the room. Elvis and his mother were asked to leave. They hadn't left me alone up until that point. One of them always stayed at my bedside, like I was gonna snatch Key and run out of the hospital. Anyway, the social worker asked me all these questions about whether I felt safe going home with Elvis and stuff like that. I told her everything. I was so thankful that somebody asked me that question. That one question saved my life—saved Key's life, because she wouldn't have been safe with that family."

"Did the social worker believe you, because I know that shit sounded crazy as hell?"

"I assume that she did because she called the police. The police located the missing person's report that True filed on me. She let me use a telephone to call *Engineered Excellence*, because it wasn't like I knew Aunt True's number without my phone.

"Once I called my aunt, you know everything else was history. She flew in and showed up at the hospital with her lawyer. They proceeded to start wrecking shit. Of course, Elvis got his own lawyer. There were a lot of back-room deals cut, basically because Elvis and his mother didn't want to be charged with kidnapping and unlawful restraint. And besides that, Elvis was a very popular pastor. He didn't want it becoming public that he'd done all of those things to me. I didn't care if they went to jail or not, to be honest. I just wanted my baby and to be able to get the hell out of that state.

"I have no idea what charges Elvis and Mrs. Emerson agreed to or if they served jail time or what. I honestly could not concentrate on them or their situation. All I cared about was my baby. The most important thing for me was that he signed away *his* parental rights to Key and agreed to stay away from her. Part of that agreement is that after her eighteenth birthday, if she asks about him or wants to meet him, he's amenable to that. But otherwise, he stays the hell away.

"But it's not like I trust him. I mean, he basically kidnapped me. What would stop him from finding Key and burning off with her? So, I keep her... hidden. I never post pictures of her on social media or let anybody else post pictures of her. I keep her to myself.

"When I say that Key is mine, she's *all* mine. Nobody else on the earth has any type of right to her or claim to her."

"Yo, run something back for me. Why wouldn't just telling Elijah her birthdate—clear up this whole 'I'm the daddy' bullshit?"

"Because Key was two months premature. Key was due in late March but born in January. Elijah and I ended in April. Nine months from April is January. So, it would look like she was his."

"You're gonna tell him that Key is actually his niece?"

"The DNA test would show a familial link, right?"

"It would."

She stared at me on the screen. "What are you thinking, Omari?"

"That it shouldn't be your job to tell him that his brother is a fucking degenerate. You're the victim here, Kitari. Those motherfuckers are the opps. First, the pussy motherfucker gets married on you and kicks you out of your own spot. Then, his even more pussy ass brother takes advantage of your heartbreak and instability by preying on you. I think you should give him the DNA test and let him figure out why Key has a familial link to him but isn't his daughter. That's not your burden to bear, sweetheart."

Her pretty brown eyes widened. "Can you imagine the narrative Elijah'll spin when he finds out? He's gonna make me out to be the biggest whore ever."

"He's not gonna make you out to be anything, because first of all, we're gonna make that loudmouth asshole sign an NDA. If he wants his brother and mother's deeds to stay secret, then he'll shut up. If not--"

"Omari, no."

"Kitari, yes. It won't be you doing him dirty. He'll make the decision. His silence in exchange for your continued silence."

"I don't know, babe. I've worked myself up to just put everything on the table."

"And I commend you for that. You're the strongest woman I know. But you don't have to do this. You don't owe him this. You don't owe him anything. His brother and mother had you locked in a house for seven months, and he never thought of you except to make sure to post foul shit about you on the internet and make sure that whenever you resurfaced, your online business would be dead. Fuck that nigga."

"But I'm supposed to talk to him tomorrow. I asked him to come early so we could talk. What reason am I supposed to give for bringing him here early, if I'm not gonna talk to him?"

"You're gonna tell him that you want him to stop talking shit about you and your daughter on the internet and otherwise, or you're gonna blow his fucking world up."

*Or I'm gonna do it for you*, I thought to myself.

# TEN

KITARI

"Everything is gonna be fine, Kit Kat. Just perfect," Aunt True assured me while patting my left hand in between both of hers.

I stared aimlessly out of the window, as we sat in the back seat of the Cadillac CT she'd hired to drive us.

My emotions were all over the place, but the most prevailing thought in mind was how thankful I was that the day had finally arrived... the day I put the Emersons behind me and behind Key.

"Even if everything goes left, it's still the day that I put these people in my rearview," I mumbled.

"Exactly. Back when Key was born, you escaped from these freaks." She whispered so that Kinzie and Key didn't hear her. "Today, you will walk away from them with your head held high, Kitari Alise. This is my word—these people will *never* have an opportunity to touch, bother, and/or mess with either you or Key again. You hear me?"

Throwing my shoulders back and sitting up straight, I exhaled a deep sigh. "I hear you, Auntie."

. . .

Our first stop of the morning was the Law Office of Rochelle, Riley, and Knight. Elijah insisted on securing the space where we would talk. He claimed that I was at an unfair advantage. Not only was Chicago my hometown, but he was in the dark about what exactly I wanted to discuss. I gave him that because I really didn't care where we talked. The location was way less important to me than getting my story out. We could've talked in the middle of the Dan Ryan Expressway for all I cared.

Elijah's attorneys were able to procure a conference room at the prestigious law firm. It would be in that designated conference room that I would tell him about Key's actual paternity and how that came to be.

I didn't expect him to believe me, not when it was my word against the word of his beloved mother and brother. Therefore, the plan was that after I'd spoken my piece, we would head over to the lab where a DNA test would be performed on both Key and Elijah.

I walked into the building with Kinzie holding True's hand, True holding mine, and me holding Key's. We were a fortress of Miller women. We didn't come to start a fight, but we damn sure came to end one.

The moment we stepped inside the lobby, we were approached by three distinguished looking black men. The tallest of the three men made a beeline for Key, scooping her up with one arm and cradling her to his chest, after which he wrapped a proprietary arm around my shoulder.

"You straight?" Omari asked me.

I tried to muscle some chest space from my daughter so both of us could share Omari.

"I'm okay." I eyeballed the shortest of the three men who'd approached us. "You brought your attorney." It was a statement, not a question.

"Hell yeah. Just in case I have to f..." He cast a side glance at Key. "Just in case Elijah Emerson has to see me."

"Kit Kat." Aunt True's voice cut through everything.

My gaze traveled over to her.

"This is Jamerson Kavanaugh, my attorney. You met him... briefly back in Londynville."

I un-plastered my body from Omari's, standing straight and extending my hand. "It's nice to see you again, Attorney Kavanaugh."

He was an older gentleman, with sharp eyes that went kind as he took me in. "It's nice to see you, too, Ms. Miller." His eyes swept over to my daughter. "And little Miss Miller, as well."

I gave him a small smile.

"Now that we're all here, we can head into the conference room," Attorney Kavanaugh informed us.

"Is Elijah already here?" I questioned.

The answer was a slight shake of the attorney's head. "According to his attorney, he's apparently been held up."

More than an hour later, Elijah still hadn't arrived. Key had grown bored with playing on my cell phone and acting silly with Kinzie. She was beginning to get restless, and I couldn't even blame her, nor did I feel like forcing her to sit still.

"This is stupid," Kinzie commented.

"Don't say stupid, Auntie Kinzie," Key admonished.

"You're right." Kinzie agreed easily. "This is d-u-m-b as h-e-l-l."

I chuckled.

"You're right, niecy pooh." True acceded. "Elijah Emerson has a lot of nerve to keep us waiting like this. Let me find Kavanaugh." Both Aunt True's attorney and Omari's had left the room to take phone calls several moments before. "If Elijah can't be here in the next ten minutes, I think we should try to get his request for a DNA test thrown out. Let him start the process over from the beginning."

"Ugh," I said softly. "I was hoping to get this over with."

"I know you were, niecy pooh, but what are we supposed to do?" She shrugged her shoulders with her hands up. "Continue to sit here and wait for another eight hours, until he deems us worthy of showing up for?"

I watched as True left the conference room, on a search for her attorney. She was right. Elijah was the pettiest man that I knew. There was no telling how long he would try to make me wait. There was no proof that he was even in Chicago, that he'd even boarded his plane.

Thirty minutes later, I was over Elijah Emerson and his shenanigans. "Kinzie, go ahead and take Key to school," I suggested.

Kinzie flicked her wrist and checked her watch.

"Is it after ten?" I questioned. Key's school had a strict policy about children not being admitted after 10:00 AM.

"Actually, it's ten forty-seven," she advised me.

My sigh was heavy. *Dayum!* I thought to myself. I couldn't even send her to school.

Kinzie took in my expression. "Don't even worry about it, Kit Kat. It's about to be a Kinzie and Key day."

My daughter looked up from where she was seated on Omari's lap, playing in his beard. Her eyes widened with interest, which Kinzie picked up on.

"That's right." She smiled and used her voice to build the excitement. "Keetyn Miller, you are going to spend the day with your BAE— Best Auntie Ever!"

Key celebrated, wiggling a dance move while remaining seated on Omari.

"First, we're gonna take an Uber to my house and pick up my car. Then, we're gonna hit the mall, where we're gonna go to Sephora and play in makeup. Maybe we'll go to Build-A-Bear and make us some forever friends. After that, we're gonna have lunch."

"Yay!" Key jumped down from Omari's lap.

"Let's go use the bathroom while we wait for our Uber."

Once Kinzie and Key headed for the bathroom, Omari and I were alone.

"How're you holding up, pretty lady?" he asked, sliding into the chair right next to mine.

"I hate waiting like this," I admitted. "I was all ready to have a... showdown, and this bastard chooses to be a *no-show*."

"You know we can leave. You responded to the petition... hell, you brought your daughter, all so he can get the test he's demanding. I feel like you've done your part. I think, at this point, at almost two hours after the agreed upon time, you can leave."

"Yeah, but if I leave now, I'll just have to come back and do this all again in a few months, when he decides to come into town. I would rather just get it over with today. I don't mind waiting today, if it means that I'll never have to deal with him ever again in life."

"And what if he never shows?"

"Well, then..." I was cut off from having to finish my thought, by True coming back into the room. Attorneys Kavanaugh and Grisham were on her heels.

"Elijah, his mother, and his attorney just arrived," True announced.

Even though it was the moment I had been waiting for, the bottom fell out of my stomach.

*Let the fuckboy games begin*, I thought to myself.

———

He'd asked to speak with me in private—just him, his mother, and me. I didn't want to speak to him in private... with his mother... without witnesses. Was he insane? The last time I'd been alone with two Emersons, I was held against my will. The last few times I'd spoken to Elijah, which had been via text, he'd talked crazy to me—called me bitches and accused me of things that weren't true. He'd spread lies about me.

"Why would you ever think that I'd be willing to speak to you and/or your mother in private?" I questioned. And that was a real question; it wasn't me being sarcastic or anything. "No."

"We all know what the situation is, Elijah." True interjected. "There's no reason to act like anything is a secret... particularly since you've been posting about the situation on social media. Why in the world would it need to be a secret now?"

In the end, we all filed into the conference room. I took a seat between True and Omari, while Elijah, his mother, and his attorney sat across from us.

"Let me..." I began, but Omari placed a calming hand on my wrist. When I looked up at him, he shook his head.

"Mr. Emerson is the petitioner," Attorney Kavanaugh elaborated from his seat on the other side of True. "He requested this hearing. Let him state his intentions."

So, I sat back and waited for Elijah to state his intentions.

"First of all, I want to apologize for my tardiness," Elijah began.

"When my mother initially told me that she would make the trip with me, I assumed it was to offer her support." He rolled his eyes at his mother, and that was when I realized that she'd told him the truth.

I wasn't sure which version of the truth she'd told him, but she must've told him enough. The look he shot her spoke volumes about how pissed he was with her.

"Instead," he continued, still glaring at her, "it was to tell me about a secret she'd been keeping for more than four years. A—"

True cut him off, shooting her own glare at Mrs. Emerson. "I hope for your sake that you told him the truth, because I was there, and so was my attorney. I'll be happy to fill in any... *holes* your story may have in it."

"And I'm happy to provide any details." I piped in, completely surprising myself because I hadn't planned on saying much of anything, particularly to Mrs. Emerson.

"I'm good," he insisted. "I don't need to hear shit else." Elijah's eyes found mine across the table. "Your daughter isn't biologically mine."

"Right. She's your niece," True clarified.

Elijah looked up at the ceiling before bringing his eyes back down, his teeth piercing his lip. "You should've just told me."

"Nah, homey. We're not doing that." Omari sat up straight, his posture going into a defensive stance.

"When was I supposed to tell you, Elijah? While you were using your team of minions to ruin me and my business? Or when you were dragging me on your socials? And why was I supposed to tell you? So you could use it against me? Post even more lies about me?"

It was at that moment that Attorney Kavanaugh slid a stack of papers across the solid wood table toward Elijah and his attorney. "Mr. Emerson, placed before you are both a cease and desist order, as well as an NDA—as nothing that is shared during this meeting may be spoken about outside of these four walls. The orders outline and detail the penalty for their violation.

"As you should have heard from your mother, Ms. Miller has been repeatedly victimized by your family. She was wrongfully evicted from her home by you, as well as slandered across various forms of media.

"Your brother and mother further victimized her by unlawfully detaining her, during which time she was impregnated by your brother. It should be mentioned that during the time that she was unlawfully detained, she was also found to be mentally impaired and was given any number of unknown prescription drugs by both your mother and your brother."

Anger started to boil inside of me. Before that moment, I had actually been feeling pretty numb. But for some reason, hearing the atrocities that had been perpetrated against me, listed by Attorney Kavanaugh, caused a hot rage to come over my entire being.

"I tried to commit suicide... twice," I said, looking directly into his eyes. "I was willing to kill myself to get away from the hell that your family caused me, and you forced me here today to claim a child that is not even yours.

"You drug me on social media and put a spotlight on my daughter because you felt like you had been wronged. All along, your sinister ass family has done nothing but wrong to me. And you have the nerve to tell me that I should have just told you? Go to hell, Elijah Emerson. You and your sick ass mother and your demented ass brother. Fuck all of y'all."

I pushed my chair back with force and stood.

"I'm suing all of you motherfuckers!" I raged. "I swear to God that I'm suing y'all for mental distress, and you." I jabbed my finger in Elijah's direction, "You, I'm suing you for slander or libel or something. I'm suing all three of you motherfuckers!" I repeated while walking toward the door of the conference room.

"You can't sue Elvis," Elijah muttered.

"Oh, his name is going at the top of the suit."

"You can't sue a dead man. He was killed in a head-on collision with an eighteen-wheeler two years ago."

That caused me to pause, but then my mouth started moving before my brain did, and I popped off. "Oh, that motherfucker is dead? Good for 'im. Hope he rots in hell!"

It had been my intention to prance out of the room, with my head held high, slamming the door behind me. What actually ended up happening, instead, was that as soon as those words left my mouth, I felt really convicted.

I stopped walking and turned to Mrs. Emerson. "I apologize for saying that. I'm sorry for your loss."

I bolted from the room.

Mere seconds later, Omari caught up with me, right before I could dip into the women's restroom.

"Kitari." He spoke my name with a gentleness I'd never heard used before in baritone. "Come here, baby."

I went willingly into his arms and pressed my face into his strong chest while I heaved sobs.

He didn't talk, just held me in silence, rubbing my back and caressing me lightly. I was thankful for the quiet. Thankful that I didn't have to explain myself. I wasn't sure that I could if I'd been asked.

All I knew was that Elijah knowing the truth and hearing that Elvis Emerson was dead had lifted a weight from my... chest... shoulders... mind? I couldn't pinpoint exactly where the stress flowed from; all I knew was that I felt free. The nightmare was really over. I no longer had to watch my back or feel that gripping fear any time Key was out of my presence.

I didn't have to worry about "one day"—the one day that Elvis decided to show up or decided to tell Key that she was his daughter. I was free. Key was free.

When Key was older and she asked about her father, I could tell her that he'd passed away with confidence. I wouldn't have to lie to my daughter in an effort to protect her from the truth or to keep her safe from the harm of coming into contact with him. He was dead. He couldn't hurt anybody else the way he'd hurt me.

"Key is free." I blubbered into Omari's chest.

"She is."

"My baby is free."

Back in the conference room, I stood and watched as Elijah signed the cease-and-desist order and the NDA paperwork. While the paperwork was handed off to an administrative assistant to make copies, Elijah approached me. My body involuntarily stiffened.

He noticed and stopped his forward motion several feet away from me. "Hey, Kitari. I owe you an apology—"

I cut him off. "You owe me waaaaayyyyy more than one apology,

Elijah. You sent me on a trip out of the country with strangers while you married somebody else. You kicked me out of my home. You ruined my livelihood. You dragged my name and my daughter's image all over and through Beyoncé's internet. You owe me a hell of a lot more than *an* apology.

"Furthermore, I will not be accepting any apologies from you, unless you give them the same way that you gave me the disrespect. You wanted to blast me and embarrass me all over social media? Then I expect your apology to be just as loud, just as strong, just as outrageous... on social media. Break the fucking internet with apologies to me and mine. Record apology videos and post them. Keep the same damn energy you had when you were dissing me. If you can't do that, then... fuck your apology!"

# EPILOGUE

## OMARI

The fans were already up on their feet. The noise level inside the stadium was deafening as the crowd counted down with the game clock. Crayden Crandon, the point guard for the Las Vegas Bighorns, had the ball, and he was bringing it up fast and furiously. I got back in position to guard my guy, but it was all fundamentals. It really didn't matter toward the outcome of the game. With only three seconds left, one bucket would still leave them four points shy of catching us.

Crayden got off his shot, but it coincided with the sounding of the buzzer and the eruption of the crowd.

The Chicago Bison had just won their fourth NBA championship in a row, and I'd just earned my very first championship ring. The feeling was euphoric. Everything about the season had been tough. Every game had been hard-won, but in that moment, every second of it was worth it for this experience.

Confetti rained down from the ceiling of the stadium. Champagne flowed. Tears flowed.

Grown men wept, some more openly than others.

Gideon Show hung around my neck. "We did it, Big Vet!" he yelled beside my ear. "We did it!"

I nodded, choking back waterworks. It felt good as hell to be a part of a winning team, and it felt even better to know I had contributed, and that my contributions were acknowledged. Before I could open my mouth to respond to Gideon, a microphone was thrust into my face. For the first time in the season, a reporter was giving me a chance at the mic.

"Omari," she said breathlessly.

She was from one of the lesser-known outlets, one that was internet-based, but it was all love. We all had to start somewhere.

"You've been in the league for thirteen years," she continued. "You've played for ten teams. Does it get any sweeter than this for you?"

"You're right." I acknowledged her comments. "I have played for a lot of different teams, in a lot of different markets, but no team has ever been like this one. No time has ever been like this one. And nah, it doesn't get any sweeter than this. We've worked hard for every basket, every free-throw, every rebound, every assist. We've worked hard, and we've earned this. The Bighorns were fierce competitors, but I'm glad that our tenaciousness and the dedication to our goal led us to come out on top."

She smiled at me gratefully. "Thanks, Omari."

Before I could thank her as well, shrieking had my ears ringing. I turned just in time to see Kitari bounding toward me, Key in her arms.

"I'm so proud of you, Big Vet!" Kitari screamed, trying to embrace me with her one free arm, but it was too short to fully embrace me. So instead, I took Key from her and gave the two of them a group hug.

Kitari reached up and pulled at my neck until I bent down. Then she placed a kiss on my lips. "I'm not saying this because you're a winner and a champion and all that. I really mean it!" she yelled.

I eyed her. "Saying what?"

"I love you," she mouthed to me.

A big ass smile crested on my face as I picked her up with my free arm, while I was still holding Key. She yelped and threw her arms around my neck, while she and Key giggled uncontrollably.

And that was the picture that went viral on Beyoncé's fucking internet.

# Epilogue II

KITARI

"Omari, stop." I swatted at his hands as he tried for the umpteenth time to grab my butt. I was partially to blame. I knew better than to walk around wearing nothing but my bra and panties, but I was trying to put on my dress. He just wouldn't let me.

"Stop? Why would I stop?" This time, he grabbed me around my waist and pulled until my body was flush against his—my back to his front.

I couldn't stop the hum of contentment from escaping my lips.

Clearly, he heard me, because a very small chuckle bubbled up in his chest. "Why're you playing hard to get, girl? You know you love this."

I did love it. I loved being wrapped up in his arms. "You're right. I would boo up with you all day... if we had the time, sir, which we do not, because the photographer is waiting on us. If I give you some, I'm gonna need to take another shower and..."

"Shhhhhhhh." The vibration of his lips tickled the shell of my ear. "Let me love up on my wife for a minute, Tari. Let me settle your spirit, baby. You're running around here like you're all alone in this and you're not."

The sigh came from deep inside of me, where the old way of doing things still must've resided. He was correct. I didn't have to do things by myself anymore. It wasn't me and Key against the world. I had a help-mate, a whole husband, and she had a dad. I relaxed into his embrace and stayed there for a minute, just enjoying the feel of him... the scent of him.

"I love you, Tari." He turned me around so that we were facing each other. "I love you," he repeated, lifting my chin with his finger, forcing eye contact.

"I love you, too," I assured him, before dipping my face into his chest.

"What's taking so long?" Key asked, bursting into the room, strug-gling with her chubby baby brother in her arms.

Omari and I looked at each other, both with a silent accusation in our eyes. "*You didn't lock the door.*" We wordlessly blamed each other.

"What did we tell you about picking him up?" I asked her, while Omari plucked our eight-month-old from our six-year old's grasp.

Key looked down at the floor. "That he's too heavy for me to be carrying."

Omari reached out and lifted Key's chin with the same finger he'd just used to lift mine. "Eyes up here, baby girl. You're not in trouble. We tell you these things so you won't hurt yourself. Locke is fat." He jiggled the rotund little boy in his arms. "We don't want you to accidentally drop him, because then you would be upset with yourself." He picked her up with his free arm and jiggled both of them.

I watched silently for a few seconds. "Key Alise, why aren't you dressed?" I probed. I'd left her dress laying across her bed, but all she had on was a slip. Yes, Key owned a slip. Her grandmother found one, some-how, somewhere.

"You aren't dressed, either," Omari pointed out, in his quest to always, always take up for Key against me. "And let my daughter live."

"Go help your daughter get dressed, sir," I commanded. "Being late for a photo shoot is bad for your image."

Ever since the photo of Omari, Key, and I at the championship game had gone viral, we'd somewhat become "media darlings." We were labeled "black love goals" and "black family goals." Everybody wanted to get pictures of us, as a family and even alone.

Of course, being the people that we were, both Omari and I shied away from the attention. But the less we gave, the more the media fought to catch. So, our wedding photos were a hot commodity, as were pictures of my pregnancy with our son, Locklen.

Him being in love with me also brought out the groupies. Women everywhere spent copious amounts of time trying to turn Omari's head, by promising him heaven between their legs. But Omari wasn't impressed or moved. He was loyal and faithful, loving and true. He was a protector and a confidante. He was... everything.

Surprisingly, one of our biggest supporters and proponents was Elijah Emerson. He never gave me that apology on social media that I required of him, but he stayed liking and hearting any posts made about Omari and me. He was always the first to comment positively about our little family unit.

Omari kissed my lips, while still holding our children in his arms. "Get dressed, pretty lady. We'll meet you downstairs in thirty."

I nodded, then watched him walk away, carrying our offspring. My heart was full. In the midst of hell, I never saw a man like Omari coming for me. But now all I could see was my better life, my better situation, my better man.

# AFTERWORD

I want to thank you again for choosing *Better Mann*.

I hope that you enjoyed the story of Kitari and Omari. If you did enjoy it, please remember to leave a review on Amazon or Goodreads.

You can also follow me on social media.
Join my Facebook group at: facebook.com/groups/425336865446902
Instagram: @authortracygray
TikTok: @authortracygray
X: @AlwaysTracyGray

# IF YOU WOULD LIKE TO READ MORE

There are several characters and couples mentioned in "Better Mann" that may have piqued your interest.

If you would like to read more about:

Christian "Cross" Upton & Genesis Cole-Upton, their book is called, ***Cross'd Up***.

Chance Parker & Kirbie Miller, their book is called, ***By Chance***.

Maddox "Busy" Mayhew, his book is called, ***Keeping Busy***.